I0590777

THE UNRELENTING FIGHTER

THE UNRELENTING FIGHTER

UNSTOPPABLE LIV BEAUFONT™ BOOK 7

SARAH NOFFKE

MICHAEL ANDERLE

This book is a work of fiction.

All of the characters, organizations, and events portrayed in this novel are either products of the author's imagination or are used fictitiously. Sometimes both.

Copyright © 2019 Sarah Noffke & Michael Anderle
Cover copyright © LMBPN Publishing
A Michael Anderle Production

LMBPN Publishing supports the right to free expression and the value of copyright. The purpose of copyright is to encourage writers and artists to produce the creative works that enrich our culture.

The distribution of this book without permission is a theft of the author's intellectual property. If you would like permission to use material from the book (other than for review purposes), please contact support@lmbpn.com. Thank you for your support of the author's rights.

LMBPN Publishing
PMB 196, 2540 South Maryland Pkwy
Las Vegas, NV 89109

First US Edition, June 2019
Version 1.01, July 2019
Print ISBN: 978-1-64202-341-1

THE UNRELENTING FIGHTER TEAM

Thanks to the JIT Readers

If I've missed anyone, please let me know!

Jeff Eaton
Jeff Goode
Nicole Emens
Micky Cocker
Crystal Wren
Larry Omans
Peter Manis
John Ashmore
Misty Roa

Editor
The Skyhunter Editing Team

For Trudy.
The first day we met, you called me a tiger.
Still my favorite college class ever. And the one that flamed my
fire for writing.
— Sarah

To Family, Friends and
Those Who Love
to Read.
May We All Enjoy Grace
to Live the Life We Are
Called.
— Michael

The pristine aquamarine water was as placid as glass, sitting between the green banks filled with lush vegetation. Behind the lake, the mountains were still covered in snow in Glacier National Park, although spring was well underway.

Liv Beaufont took a calming breath, enjoying the beauty all around her. A cursory glance at the water showed her image: her hood pulled over her head and an elf-made axe in her hands.

She sensed the monster at her back a second before she smelled him. Timing was important since the beasts could move fast when they wanted to. Liv tightened her grip on the axe, brought it back behind her head, spun around, and launched it at the demon speeding in her direction. The weapon flew through the air, plunging straight into the monster's forehead and nearly splitting it in two. The demon's black blood splattered the dainty white flowers littering the grass underfoot.

Unfortunately, the blow wasn't enough to stop the

monster. It lumbered forward, its arms reaching, the axe protruding grossly from its red forehead.

Liv whipped Bellator from its sheath and brought it around and down to slice the demon's midsection. The scream that escaped the beast's mouth echoed through the valley, making Liv squint from the high-pitched sound.

The demon fell in her direction, but Liv dove out of the way, staying safely on the bank. Water splashed Liv's boots and cloak as the demon dropped into it, the black blood staining the lake instantly and overtaking the once-clear blue. The waters rippled from the disturbance, spreading out around the sinking body.

Shaking her head, Liv clicked her tongue in disappointment. "Damn demons have to ruin everything."

She didn't tense when Stefan Ludwig arrived at her side soundlessly, moving even faster than the demon she'd just slain.

"Look what it did to the flowers," he remarked.

Casually, Liv glanced over her shoulder to where the demon's blood had splattered the sweet little white flowers. "I think you should clean that up. Those tourists we passed ten miles back might be catching up with us soon."

Stefan yawned, stretching his hands over his head. "They were mortals. They won't see it for what it is."

Liv agreed with a nod. "Yeah, they'll probably think a water buffalo or a moose fell into the lake."

"Do they have water buffalos in these parts?" Stefan asked, rubbing his hands over his stubbled cheeks.

Liv shrugged. "Honestly, this is my first time in Montana. I think there are a few loose minotaurs still in Glacier National Park, but they aren't enough of a problem for the council to assign a Warrior to round them up."

Stefan sighed, looking longingly at the vast beauty around them. "Maybe I'll be lucky enough to get that case if it comes up."

Raising a curious eyebrow at him, Liv shook her head. "You're *the* demon hunter. The council knows that. They aren't even questioning your unprecedented success rates anymore."

"I don't know," Stefan replied. "I think they are, which is why they sent you along to assist me. Maybe they are curious to see if you'll slow me down."

"Why would I do that?" Liv questioned. "We have a great system. You track down the demons, and I kill them." She lifted Bellator, summoning a handkerchief to clean the demon's blood from the blade. "I do have a weapon that makes the job easier."

"Yes, that's true," Stefan said, sighing again. "But they don't know that. Maybe they're hoping our reports won't line up, or that the readings on our magic use will tell them how I slaughter so many demons so fast. Or maybe they're hoping you'll rat on me. Divulge my secrets."

Liv's gaze fell to Stefan's arm, where the master demon Sabatore had bitten him. "You're insane. There's no way I would do that, but your other theories are plausible."

"I don't think they know what to do with you presently," Stefan admitted. "You sort of surprised them with that whole working for Father Time business. I don't think any Warrior has ever gone over the council's head like that. Actually, before Father Time showed up, there wasn't any official who ranked higher than the council."

"In the made-up world of justice the council lives in, you mean," Liv corrected, sheathing Bellator.

"Well, they are the ruling force in the magical world," Stefan said with another sigh.

"Because they say so." Liv summoned the axe to her, holding it away from her since the demon's blood still dripped from the blade. It had been a gift from Renswick Shoshaw-nawalla, the elf who had helped to heal Stefan. He'd apparently shut up the gothic home where he had lived in Ashland, Oregon and started a trip around the world, telling Liv that he was tired of living as a recluse, in fear of demons. In truth, he'd been freed after the incident with Stefan, and also knew the streets around the world were now safer with the demon hunter on the loose, rounding up the evil beasts. Still, they all knew that Stefan wasn't invincible, although he seemed like it.

"Someone has to elect themselves the rulers of magic, don't you think?" Stefan asked, a smile tucked at the corner of his mouth. He was playing devil's advocate because he knew it riled Liv up.

She rolled her eyes at him, cleaning off the axe and sheathing it as well. "Yes, and if everything the House of Seven did protected justice, I guess it would be okay." Again, she fought the urge to tell him about the mortal Seven and the House of Fourteen. It was getting more difficult as they grew closer, and she inherently knew she could trust him. However, Stefan had his own burdens, and currently, they seemed to be displayed on his features, weighing him down.

"So, this need for a new case," she began, trying to change the subject. "Where did it come from? I thought you enjoyed demon hunting? Well, when it wasn't keeping you from sleeping or having a single peaceful moment, that is."

Stefan's laughter echoed across the water, which was starting to settle after the demon's disturbance. "I've taken up meditation."

"Does it help any with the constant urge to hunt down evil and banish it from the world?"

He shook his head. "No, but I'm a little cooler on crowded streets, not mouthing off to inconsiderate pedestrians."

"Maybe *I* should meditate, then."

He arched a single eyebrow at her. "We both know you'll need more than meditation to keep that temper at bay."

"Axe-throwing helps," Liv said, patting her belt where the axe was. "There's something about flinging an axe through the air and having it stick into a target that is very satisfying."

"Let me guess," Stefan said with a grin. "You didn't play with dolls growing up, did you?"

Liv shot him a look of offense. "Of course I did. What else was I going to blow up?"

He laughed, some of his stress from before melting away. "To be honest, I do enjoy demon hunting, but it's starting to get old. I want to do something that challenges me in different ways. Something where I can use other skills."

"Other skills?" Liv questioned.

"Yeah, like my brains and personality," he responded,

then quickly added, "And yes, I have those. I'm not just a pretty face."

Liv shrugged. "I thought you were just a brute who slaughtered demons and laughed at my jokes even though they soared over your head."

He feigned hurt. "I'm a real person, Liv. And it's about time you notice that. I actually have feelings."

"Like, how many feelings?" she bantered.

"At least two," he answered without missing a beat. "Hunger and rage."

She nodded. "Then we are absolutely the same, Warrior Ludwig."

"Oh, I don't know. Every now again, when you don't think anyone is looking, I daresay you're happy," Stefan observed.

Liv yanked out her axe, clutching it menacingly in her hand. "You take that back, or pay the price."

Stubbornly, he shook his head. "Do your worst to me. I'm certain I deserve it, Warrior Beaufont. And if I'm brutally honest with you, having you accompany me on these cases sort of, kind of, marginally, makes me happy. At least, it seems to make the part of me bent on abolishing evil relax a bit."

For a moment, Liv didn't know what to say. There was such earnestness in his voice. Finally, she recovered, clearing her throat uncomfortably. "Are you sure you have a good grasp of the English language? By happy, do you actually mean indifferent? And when you say I relax that part of you, I think you mean that I distract you with my quirky behavior and rebellious nature."

"You say potato," Stefan countered. For a moment, Liv thought he was going to say something else, a meaningful expression flickering behind his eyes. She wasn't sure she could handle whatever he confessed next, which was why she was strangely grateful when his head jerked up in that way it always did when he caught a whiff of something evil.

"Where is it?" Liv asked, scanning the area around them, enjoying the adrenaline that made her heart speed up. It was an old, familiar feeling before a hunt.

"I'm not sure," he answered, completing his circle. "Something's not right."

Liv tensed at the caution in Stefan's voice. Demons never scared him. Not anymore. They had few advantages over him. He was immune to their bite, and he was stronger than them, having inherited all their powers without any of their disadvantages. But suddenly his usual confidence had vanished, replaced by an uncharacteristic fear. "Not right, how?" Liv asked, worry in her voice despite her efforts to mask it.

"I can sense the vermin, but I can't find them, which is weird," Stefan said, cutting his eyes at her. "Get Bellator out. We don't have time for fancy and fun axe action this time."

Liv wanted to laugh. Even though danger was seemingly approaching, Stefan's casual, amusing demeanor was still present, entertaining her. She sheathed the axe and pulled out Bellator, feeling it warm in her hands. It tugged down at the ground under their feet. Her gaze shot to the grassy patch just as two red hands shot through the dirt and wrapped around Stefan's feet, yanking him into the ground. The dirt opened up so fast, buckling in two, that it knocked Liv onto her back.

She rolled over at once, trying to figure out what was going on. Dirt sprayed up in all directions. Screams filled the air, both Stefan's and those of a demon. The earth rocked underfoot, making it difficult to get closer. And as Liv approached, her feet sank, like she was venturing into quicksand.

Stefan was being sucked into the ground, and soon he'd be gone. His hands flailed in the air as his gurgled screams faded slightly. Liv looked around for something to help him, but there were only pretty white flowers and dirt. She needed a vine. Since there was nothing of the sort, Liv sheathed Bellator and summoned a rope, pulling it from where it was lying on her desk in her apartment.

"Heads up!" she yelled, swinging the rope over her head and throwing it to Stefan. It flew through the air, only grazing through his hands before she pulled it back to her. Two more times, she threw it. His hands were nearly buried. They were running out of time.

With her heart nearly beating out of her chest, she tried one more time. The rope tugged in her hands when he caught it, his fingers gripping tightly. Liv yanked, but it did no good. Stefan was being pulled underground. His head was practically covered. To his side, she could see movement. The demon. Or demons. They were tugging him under. Burying him deep in the ground where he couldn't fight them or survive.

Liv knew she had to act fast. Tying the rope around her waist, she pulled out Bellator, watching the movement of the dirt carefully. Where Stefan was, it moved frantically—

a result of his panic. To the side of him, it rippled—as though the demon was swimming deeper, kicking to make room for them as they headed toward the core of the Earth.

Taking a deep breath, Liv issued a silent prayer. *Please don't let me kill him.*

Then she plunged Bellator into the dirt, and it met flesh. She hesitated. A high-pitched scream she'd heard too many times and associated with demons came from under the ground. That was the confirmation she needed. Liv pushed the sword in deeper, and the dirt around Bellator stilled.

The area around Stefan moved more wildly. Holding onto the rope around her waist, Liv yanked. Relief filled her chest when Stefan's head broke the surface like a worm in a garden. She continued to yank, working fast, sweat flooding her face. She was worried that more demons were hiding under the ground, ready to finish the job the first demon had started.

Stefan spat out dirt when his face broke free, covered in soil. Furiously he climbed out of the hole, releasing the rope and crawling as quickly as he could manage away from it. When he was at Liv's feet, he turned on his back and crab-walked farther away, his eyes crazed with worry as he regarded the giant hole that had materialized only moments prior.

When nothing erupted out of it to attack them, Stefan, strangely, laughed out loud.

Concerned that he'd lost his mind, Liv turned to him, aware that she was putting her back to the opening. "Are you okay?"

He nodded, pushing up to his feet. From head to toe, he was caked with moist dirt. "I'm fine," he said, still sounding amused. "But just when I think I've got those damn demons figured out, they change their tactics and come after me a different way."

Liv shook her head at him, wiping Bellator off. "And here you said you were getting bored with demon hunting."

"Not bored," he corrected. "I simply said I wanted a different kind of challenge."

"Well, you nearly became a buried corpse," Liv stated. "Guess they figured out that biting you was ineffective, but suffocating you in dirt would definitely do the trick."

Stefan dusted off his cloak, which did little good since it was thoroughly covered. "Yes, a good reminder that there are other ways a demon could kill me if they wanted to."

Liv shook her head at the hole, still holding Bellator at the ready. "Are they gone?"

Stefan considered this and then nodded, striding over to where the dead demon lay just below the surface of the Earth. He toed it, exposing the monster's black blood. "Yes, and your quick thinking about stabbing blindly into the dirt to kill that demon definitely saved my life. Another minute and I would have been gone."

"I didn't stab blindly," Liv stated. "Bellator can sense these things, and I was paying attention to how the ground was moving. Above you, it was all erratic since you were having a hissy fit."

"Right. Hissy fit. But if that had been Liv Beaufont, she'd be telling jokes and probably yawning," Stefan joked.

"I doubt that," she said. "I had a double espresso earlier.

But definitely telling jokes, or at least seriously insulting the damn demon."

"I'm glad you are attuned to Bellator well enough to follow its lead."

"Because that saved your life?" she asked.

"Because one day it will save yours," he stated. "And yes, thanks for coming to my rescue once again."

"Don't mention it," she said with a wink.

"Oh, I will mention it," he retorted. "If I didn't know any better, I'd say you want me to stick around for a long time."

"At least long enough to return the favor."

Holding out a dusty arm, Stefan offered it to her. "How about I start by buying you a drink?"

Liv nodded. "Yeah, I could use one. But if you think I'm taking your arm, Mud Cakes, you're absolutely wrong."

He smiled, the lines around his mouth filled with dirt. "I prefer 'Warrior Mud Cakes.'"

CHAPTER TWO

The younger brother reluctantly strode through the darkness of the Black Void. Adler swung around, his hostility palpable.

"Would you keep up?" he fired at Decar.

"I'm trying," he lied, his pale eyes sliding around, worry evident in them. This wasn't a place that lent a person confidence. It smelled horrid. The void was filled with the strange rhythmic breaths of the God Magician. And there was a sinister feel that wrapped around anyone who entered the space, weakening them. This was one of the God Magician's tactics for ensuring he had the upper hand when in another's company. And he was definitely getting stronger, given the intensity of the feeling.

It wasn't just Decar's very vocal hesitation about seeing the God Magician that had put Adler in a sour mood. Sure, that was part of it. Adler didn't like entering this space or dealing with the One and his ever-growing temper either, but things had to be done.

However, Adler was also stressed because his dragon

companion Indikos had disappeared. This wasn't like him. Nothing Adler did brought the miniature dragon to him, and he couldn't understand it. He consoled himself with the fact that he'd successfully stolen Sophia's dragon's egg. *Maybe that was it,* Adler pondered as he trod forward, stepping over the bones of small animals. Indikos might be worried that the dragon which hatched from the egg would replace him. He was jealous.

Adler smiled to himself. A little competition was never a bad thing. He held up his staff, the glowing orb on the top both lighting the way and illuminating something on the ground ahead. Whatever it was moved like water, flowing on the stone floor.

After three more steps, Adler halted, revulsion filling his stomach. Snakes. Hundreds of hissing snakes covered the floor, all headed for the man sitting on the stone throne ahead. Although the light didn't reach him, it was easy to make out the God Magician's features since his eyes were two strobes of light, illuminating everything around him and especially that which he looked at.

When he glanced at Adler and Decar, they both shielded their faces from the bright lights which had instantly made their eyes water and sting.

"You brought your brother," Talon Sinclair observed, studying Decar.

Adler dropped to one knee, bowing to his oldest living relative. Well, the oldest magician to ever live. "Yes, my Lord. As you requested." He angled his head in Decar's direction, urgency in his glare. His brother took the hint, copying Adler's stance.

"Master, it is an honor to finally be in your presence,"

Decar said in a breathless voice, partially covering his nose because of the smell.

"Stand and let me have a look at you," the God Magician ordered, his voice echoing in their chests. He had gotten stronger, Adler realized. That was how he had been able to summon the snakes, which Adler realized after closer inspection had tiny legs. Visibly Adler shivered, watching as the serpents slithered around the One's feet, crawling over the throne and finding a resting place behind or around the God Magician.

Talon's gaze shone on Decar, making him clench his eyes closed as he attempted to keep his hands by his side. "Yes, you're an albino like me. They like to call it an abnormality, but what makes us different makes us superior."

"M-M-My Lord," Decar sputtered, his tone pleading.

"Tell me about your progress, Decar," the God Magician ordered.

"I've been tracking the giant known as Bermuda Laurens, as you ordered," Decar began, his eyes still closed because of the One's unrelenting gaze on him. "She is definitely searching for information about how the history was erased."

"And has she learned anything or communicated it to anyone?" Talon asked.

Decar shook his head. "No, not that I'm aware of."

"I do not dwell in the world of assumptions!" the One boomed, his voice making the walls vibrate. Dust rained down on them from the unseen ceiling. "You're as useless as Adler if you think this is at all satisfactory."

Decar bowed his head, his hands shaking by his sides. "I'm sorry. I meant to say that she has not."

Talon let out a long, satisfied sigh as more serpents crawled onto his arms and legs. "And why haven't you gotten rid of this giant yet?"

"I've tried, my Lord," Decar explained. "She has eluded me, but I know I can take her out as you ordered. I only need a little more time."

"If she," Talon began, his words terse, "succeeds and finds out the truth, it will be you who pays the price. I have worked for too long to have one giant ruin everything."

"I understand, Father," Decar said, his tone still pleading. "I won't allow that to happen."

"We will see." Talon's gaze swiveled to Adler, instantly blinding him but giving Decar some relief. "And you… When do you leave for the Matterhorn?"

"Very soon, Father," Adler said, his eyes watering from the intensity of the light. "I simply have a few more affairs to put in order."

"If you delay much longer and that girl gets to the Matterhorn again, it will jeopardize everything," Talon hissed.

Adler nodded. "I understand, my Lord. I will be quick."

"What is it that delays you?" the God Magician asked.

Adler couldn't tell him he was looking for Indikos, or that he was afraid of leaving Talon alone in the House of Seven. However, soon the God Magician would be strong enough to break into his thoughts. "Well, you asked me to track down Father Time."

"And have you?" Talon asked.

"No, but Olivia Beaufont knows where he is," he explained. "I'm hoping she'll lead me to him."

A laugh that sounded more like a cry echoed from the

God Magician's mouth. "My old nemesis Father Time will sense that I'm alive soon, but it will be too late. I'll be strong enough, and can finally rid this world of him."

Adler shivered again. It wouldn't be long until Talon was at full strength. Then everything would change. That was what all the preparations had been for, but now that it was happening, it felt like too much. Still, he'd come too far to abandon the mission. And he wanted what the God Magician had promised him: immortality. Just like his ancient relative, he'd live forever. They'd rule side by side, having obliterated the other families in the House.

Talon had only kept the royal blood of the other six families alive so that he could come back one day. Once he was at full strength, they'd be wiped out like the others and their power would be given to Adler, preserving him forever. Everything had actually worked out perfectly.

The God Magician might scare the hell out of Adler, but he was by far the most ingenious man to ever live. He'd won a war, forced the mortals out of the House, changed history, and figured out how to live forever using the holy power of the families from the House of Seven.

"Go and find me Father Time," Talon ordered. "Only once he's dead can I rise fully from my crypt."

Adler bowed, reveling in the fact that Olivia Beaufont had drawn Father Time out of hiding. If she hadn't, then they could never finish things and finally rule over the magical world for the rest of their immortal lives. Father Time would try to stop them. However, everything had changed when Olivia Beaufont informed the council that Father Time was back. She'd thought she was so smug, working directly for the gnome. Little did she know that was exactly what Adler needed.

Centuries ago, when Talon was ready to rise to full power and take over the House, Father Time had disappeared. That had halted everything, which was why the House of Seven had stayed intact, the blood of the Royals keeping it going. However, soon those other families would no longer be necessary. Once Father Time was dead, there would be no stopping the Sinclairs from ruling the magical world.

CHAPTER THREE

"This thing is more stubborn than it needs to be," John grumbled, wiping sweat off his face as he shook his head at the pinball machine.

"I think many a person has said the same about me," Liv kidded, offering Pickles a treat. The little terrier twirled around on his hind legs, showing his delight. Plato, apparently not thinking the little dance was all that cute, rolled his eyes from the countertop on which he resided.

"Those who say that about you simply don't understand you. You're better off without those negative influences in your life," John offered.

"Well, unfortunately, I can't kick the council out of my life, or half the other jerks that I run into on a regular basis either," Liv replied. "But hey, they keep me humble. Or at least, that's what I like to tell myself."

She pulled another treat out of the bag and offered one to Plato. His nose jerked up straight into the air with supreme repulsion. "So, I'll take that as a 'no' to the treat," Liv said to the lynx.

"That cat of yours is as ornery as this machine," John remarked.

"And he talks," Liv said at once.

"I'll believe it when I hear it," he fired back.

Liv sighed, knowing Plato was never going to indulge her and make a peep in John's presence. It had become a matter of pride at this point. "So, you still can't figure out what is wrong with that pinball machine?"

John shook his head at the Wonder Wizard Demolition Derby Pinball Machine. "No, and the sad part is that I have a very interested buyer. The deal is done, but the machine has to be working."

"Well, we're going to figure out what the issue is. Then I'll repair it using my hocus pocus, and you'll be off to Barbados or Hawaii or wherever you've picked for your dream vacation."

Running his hand through what little gray hair he had left on his head, John didn't look as confident. "I think I'd rather go up north to some cabin in the woods. Maybe Washington or Utah or Montana."

Liv shivered, seeing a flash of the recent situation involving Stefan in Glacier National Park. "I've just gotten back from Montana. Stay away."

"Oh? Lots of tourists this time of year?" John asked. "I get enough of those in West Hollywood. No, thanks."

"There were a good number of tourists in the national park, but also a fair number of demons."

"Oh, double no, thanks," John stated. "I think I saw one of those during my stint overseas."

"That's because you can see magic," Liv explained. "Most mortals don't see demons for what they are. They make up a plausible excuse or just get a bad feeling. However, your founder's blood makes you different. Better."

"I'm not so sure about that," John said with a sigh.

Liv knew he wasn't entirely convinced he was one of the mortal Seven. She wasn't either, but it made the most sense. And maybe deep down, she just *wanted* him to be one of the Seven so that they could one day go to work together. She laughed to herself, thinking of them closing up shop here in the evening and then commuting over to the House of Seven…or rather, Fourteen.

The council needed people like John. He was rational and caring and didn't just think about the greater good. John Carraway wanted what was right for the individual as well. He wanted a sustainable future, which was why he owned an electronic repair shop instead of selling brand-new shiny devices to people that would break in a year and fill up the landfills.

"You know, demons are pretty much like tourists," Liv said, sensing she needed to change the subject.

As she suspected, that did the trick, brightening John's face. "Oh, yeah? How's that?"

"Well, both smell funny, are way too loud, and only care about what they want to experience," Liv explained.

John chuckled. "I think we are just jaded by having been in this part of LA for so long. But you're right. The tourists do seem to insist upon their own agendas, as if the rest of us don't have our own lives to live."

"And yet, they are a part of the lifeblood of this city." Liv let out a long breath.

John went to push up from the floor, groaning from the

simple task. Liv extended a hand to him, but he shook his head.

"Don't be like the pinball machine and Plato," Liv warned. "Take my hand, old man."

He laughed at that, taking her hand and allowing her to help him up. "Thanks. I guess I could use a vacation. These bones aren't what they used to be."

Liv shook her head at him. "That's just stuff you tell yourself."

"No, that's what the doctor tells me, too," John replied. "He says I have the beginning symptoms of arthritis." He flexed his fingers, paying great attention to them as they slowly moved back into place. "I'm not a magician like you, made to withstand a few hundred years on this Earth."

Liv didn't like where this conversation was going. Yes, mortals didn't live as long and didn't have access to magic, but they were important for the balance. She just knew it.

Sensing her worry, he waved her off. "Anyway, how's the other job going?"

He asked this casually, as if referring to a part-time gig waiting tables at La Boheme.

Liv stretched her hands over her head. "It's good. And by good, I mean it's confounding my brain with too many mysteries. I recovered my mother's sword, Inexorabilis. However, I've got to find the elf who made it to access the memories locked inside. And then there's the whole 'unraveling who is behind this cover-up of the mortal Seven business. Probably Adler, but I don't want to make assumptions. He might just be a grumpy jerk who hates jokes and thinks I should die for my awful fashion sense. And then there are the cases, which are probably stacking up as we speak. But other than that, I'm feeling a lot of job satisfaction and have no new complaints for human resources, which incidentally doesn't exist in the House of Seven."

"That's worrisome," John stated.

"Yeah, it's definitely a violation if someone finds out," Liv imparted. "There are a myriad of issues. Worker's compensation issues, overtime problems, discrimination. Not to mention the hostile work environment."

John chuckled. "With everything you've got going on, I have to think that you should be at the House or working these side cases and not here."

Liv shook her head. "How many times have we been through this?"

"Well, my memory isn't as good as yours, so I'll call it an even dozen."

"Fourteen," Liv corrected. "I want to help with the pinball machine. And repairing Mrs. Jones' vacuum cleaner. And everything else that gets brought through that door."

"But how are you going to accomplish everything you need and still help me?" John asked.

"I don't know, but that isn't your concern," Liv said, trying to sound sensitive yet as firm as possible. John was trying to help, but pushing Liv away from what she loved most wasn't going to accomplish that. "What I need from you is to figure out what's wrong with the pinball machine so I can repair it. Then pack your swim trunks, because you're setting sail for your first vacation in over thirty years."

"And who is going to watch the shop?" John asked.

Liv looked around like the answer was written on the walls. "I don't know. I will, with the assistance of Rory and Plato and who knows who else."

John smiled. "Well, then I guess I better find out what's wrong with this machine."

Liv winked at him. "Yeah, you better."

CHAPTER FOUR

Although it was absolutely necessary, Liv didn't like what she was going to have to do next.

She entered the apartment Clark and Sophia shared, expecting to see the little girl playing in the middle of the living area. Well, playing in the way the little magician did, which usually involved bewitching her dolls so they put on a show for her or played Sardonza, a kid's game that magicians loved.

Instead, the living room was empty, but it felt like it was bursting with emotions. Maybe Liv was only transferring her own emotions onto the place filled with furniture from her childhood. It was arranged differently than it had been in the apartment she'd shared with her parents and siblings, but it still felt the same as when she left the House of Seven. Like it was full of their ghosts.

Her eyes flicked to the writing across the main wall. It had been in her old home too. It made her proud that Clark had ensured the words were written here: *Familia Est Sempiternum.*

"Yes, it is," Liv said in a whisper, headed for Sophia's room.

Liv was surprised to find Clark kneeling and looking up at the little girl when she entered.

"Are you sure it's him?" Clark asked. He was wearing a tan suit and a gray bow tie. It was like he enjoyed being uncomfortable, Liv thought.

Sophia similarly was dressed. She looked like she was going to the horse races in a poofy emerald dress with white lace at the hem. "Yes, I know intuitively it's him. I can feel it in a way that's hard to explain."

"Who is 'him?'" Liv asked, sliding into the room.

The little girl's face brightened at the sight of her sister and she ran over, wrapping her arms around Liv's waist and hugging her fiercely. Liv thought she would bowl her over with her strength. "Hey there!" she said with a laugh. "What have they been feeding you lately?"

Sophia released her, looking up with a proud expression. "It's probably my sessions with Akio. He has me doing conditioning exercises. I had to hold a plank for two minutes."

In contrast to her siblings, Liv looked like a homeless ninja. She was dressed in all black, her pants ripped from when she was sparring with the asshole demon in Montana. The cloak on her shoulders was still singed at the edges from when she was practicing her fireball magic, which apparently could ricochet off a brick wall in the back alley of the repair shop and chase her. She had learned this the hard way.

"Oh, yes," Liv related. "That man and his planks. They

are the bane of my existence, but what a Takahashi fighter tells us to do, we should do."

Clark shook his head. "Are you sure Akio doesn't suspect anything? I'm not sure I'm comfortable with him training Soph in combat."

Liv shook her head. "She's next in line to be Warrior. It's common for those in her position to start training about now. And don't worry; although I realize that just by saying those words, you had three mini-panic attacks. Worry as much as will make you feel comfortable, dear brother."

"Guess what, Liv?" Sophia said excitedly.

"Ummm…I'm super bad at this game and usually loathe when people ask me that, but for you, Soph, I'll play. Is it that Clark has decided that bowties are cool and added them to his collection?"

Sophia shook her head of blonde ringlets.

"Bianca Mantovani got her nose stuck in a ceiling vent, but that hasn't deterred her from being the biggest snob in the magical world?"

Clark rolled his eyes. Sophia giggled.

"All right, here's my last guess," Liv stated, thinking hard. "Adler got a buzz cut because he's tired of having to shampoo and condition those gorgeous white locks of his, but now he regrets the decision and is sporting an awesome red wig."

"How do you even come up with this stuff?" Clark asked, looking slightly amused.

"It's a gift," Liv stated.

"Adler wearing a red wig," Sophia said, overcome by laughter.

"You know he wants to see what he'd look like with colored hair," Liv said. "And red would match his complexion."

"That's not what I was going to tell you, though," Sophia stated. "I've been communicating with my dragon, and know he's somewhere in the House."

Liv's jovial demeanor dropped. "Are you serious? That's wonderful, Soph. Did he roll away? Has he hatched?"

Clark held up his hand. "Now, we don't know for sure that what Sophia's hearing is real or actually her dragon."

Liv shot him a disgusted look. "She says it is, then it is. And she communicated with the dragon before when he wanted you all to turn off the lights and keep it quiet."

Lowering his chin, Clark gave her a cautious glare in a way that Sophia couldn't see the intent in his eyes. "Don't you think it's possible that imagination is coming into play here?"

"No," Liv said flatly. "And just because you don't have any imagination, that's no reason to dismiss what Sophia is experiencing as not real."

Clark huffed. "I'm not. I just think that we need to be careful with all this."

Liv dismissed him, kneeling so she was even with Sophia. "What did the dragon say? Besides that, he's still in the House."

"He says he was taken," Sophia said earnestly. "He doesn't know where he is or who took him, but he didn't roll away."

"Someone came in here, then," Liv said, looking around the room. She'd suspected as much but hadn't wanted to believe it until it was confirmed. "How did they know about the dragon's egg? And how were they able to get in here? Only Beaufonts can enter this apartment."

Clark cleared his throat in the way he did when he was about to "explain" things. "Although the House rules dictate that only those of the family can enter their dwellings unless invited, there are certain provisional clauses that allow this rule to be broken."

"Which are?" Liv asked.

"Things related to cleaning, maintenance, and renovations of the space," Clark stated.

"So what you're saying is there are loopholes," Liv gathered.

He nodded.

"Sophia, keep communicating with your dragon. Ask him to listen for clues or anything else that can help us to determine where he is," Liv ordered.

The young magician nodded adamantly. "I'm already on it. He says he was asleep when he was taken, so he didn't hear anything. Currently, he's in a place that is warm and dark, but he hasn't been able to find any other clues."

"And I guess hatching and slaying the person who stole him is out of the question," Liv posed.

Sophia giggled. "Although that would fix one problem, I wouldn't be there for the hatching, and that's really important."

Liv nodded, understanding at once. "Well, don't worry. We're going to find Herbert."

Clark grimaced. "Herbert?"

"I'm trying out names for Sophia's dragon," Liv stated. "We can't keep calling him 'the dragon.' That will get confusing, and it's a bit impersonal."

"Because there are so many other dragons around that we'll confuse him with?" Clark asked.

Sophia giggled. "I like Herbert, but I don't think it will fit."

"We'll keep running through options," Liv assured her. "Maybe there is a baby dragon name book in the library."

It was good to see Sophia laugh. Liv had been pained when the little girl lost her egg. Watching her cry had been heartbreaking. Then she'd presented her with Inexorabilis, and that had mended things some. But now she was going to have to disappoint her sister, and that was excruciatingly difficult.

"Hey, Soph," Liv began carefully. "I'm going to need to borrow Inexorabilis."

The disappointment that fell on the young magician's face made Liv speak more rapidly.

"It's not for long, I promise. And I will be extremely careful with it. I wouldn't take it if it wasn't absolutely necessary, but it's the only way to find the elf who made it."

Sophia's expression softened as she nodded. "It's okay, Liv. I totally understand. It's been nice to have it close by, but it's more important to find out what memories Mommy locked into the sword."

Liv lightened with relief. "Thank you. I agree. Once we know that information, we'll make incredible progress."

"Actually, I was going to recommend you take the sword anyway," Clark cut in. "If someone can get into our apartment, we need to be careful about what we have in here. We aren't supposed to have Mother's sword, and if someone knew we did, they'd piece together a lot more."

Liv nodded as Sophia went and retrieved the sword

from her dresser. "Yes, so I'll work on finding the maker. You, Clark, figure out how to protect your home. And Sophia, let's find your dragon's egg."

The other siblings approved of this plan at once. As they chatted about the details, they had no idea that hiding under Sophia's bed was Indikos, Adler Sinclair's miniature dragon. He hadn't moved from that spot since helping Adler find and steal the dragon's egg. He wasn't sure when the right time to come out and help the Beaufonts was.

Many times he'd doubted if he was doing the right thing by betraying his master, and yet, it was Adler who had done something so unspeakable in the dragon world that the path should be clear. No one was to ever come between a dragon and their rider. That was sacred, and Adler knew it. Working for his own selfish gain had gone too far this time, and that was not something Indikos could overlook.

CHAPTER FIVE

"Is it my imagination, or is the Black Void bigger today?" Liv asked Plato as they stood between The Chamber of the Tree and the residential wing of the House of Seven.

The lynx tilted his head to the side and squinted one eye. "Maybe. But it could just be your imagination."

"I remember when I thought *you* were just a figment of my imagination," Liv stated.

"And have you firmly concluded that I'm not?" he asked.

"Depends on the day," Liv replied. "When you turned into a griffin to save me, I think that really swayed the factors."

"I don't recall that happening," Plato said coolly. "How much did you have to drink during this alleged incident?"

"Remember when you saved me after I fell off the side of the Matterhorn and flew me down to safety."

Plato shook his head. "Not ringing any bells. Sounds like you had elevation sickness and hallucinated. Common problem that magicians have."

"No, it's not," she fired back, turning to face the Door of

Reflection. "I don't know why you have to be so coy with me."

"It's part of my charm."

"Is it?" Liv questioned. "I'm not sure it's working for me."

"Well, it's working for me."

Liv strode for the Door of Reflection and halted, something suddenly occurring to her. She swung around to face Plato. "Is that it? If you tell your secrets, do you lose them?"

His eyes slid to the side.

"But if that *is* true," Liv continued when he didn't answer, "it means you can't answer that question. You can't tell me anything, which is about right."

Still Plato remained silent.

What had Bermuda's book said about lynxes? Something about how they hid the truth? Maybe the truth was part of Plato's power, and if he revealed it, that took away from who he was. It would explain why he'd never told her he was omniscient and omnipresent and could change into multiple different cat-related things. However, it still didn't explain why he detested Rory's kittens. More questions.

"Okay, well, I'm going to go and face the council since apparently the cat's got your tongue," Liv stated.

"Ha-ha," Plato said humorlessly.

"Oh, you like that one, do you?" Liv asked. "Well, I just happen to have many more cat clichés for you on the way."

"I. Cannot. Wait."

Liv shook her head, facing back toward the Door of Reflection. "Oh, I sense your sarcasm, but that's fine. When it comes to expert joke telling, I can't be deterred."

"Don't quit your day jobs," Plato said as she stepped through the mirror.

Liv thought she'd be prepared for the carnage or heartbreak the Door of Reflection served up to her from her subconsciousness. However, what she saw when she stepped through the door wasn't what she expected, and it therefore knocked her off balance.

Standing in the middle of a dark, nondescript room was a much older version of Liv. She had known for a while what she'd look like when she aged because she'd seen that image in a hand mirror she'd looked into in Papa Creola's shop. Still, looking at her older self was disconcerting. Worse than that was the state of her appearance. She wore the same clothes she had on presently, although they were seriously worn, like she'd never taken them off.

"How could I have not figured any of it out?" the older version of Liv stated in a morose voice, tears close to the edge. In her hands, she held Inexorabilis.

"I never found the sword's maker, or the truth, or who was behind all this," she said to the darkness before falling to her knees, the sword clanging to the ground in front of her. Crying now, Liv covered her face, shaking her head. "I failed my parents. I failed my family. I failed everyone."

Unable to watch a moment more of the self-pity, which was so unlike Liv, she stepped through the Door of Reflection, grateful to be in the Chamber of the Tree, even if Adler was giving her a sharp look of disapproval.

Decar was absent, as usual. Liv had no idea what cases he was ever assigned. Probably something fun that didn't endanger his life. Where was the fun in that? Maria Rosario was being addressed by the council when Liv took her spot next to Stefan. She was surprised to see him there since his cases were always the same: kill demons.

"It is most disappointing that you weren't able to make any progress with the elf negotiations," Lorenzo said.

"I honestly tried," Maria began, but Adler cut her off, holding up his hand.

"Your efforts simply didn't work," he stated. "We need someone who can get the elves to agree to our terms. Anything short of that is unsatisfactory."

"Yes, maybe someone who has shown exemplary skills working with other races," Raina Ludwig offered, winking at Liv.

"That would be ideal," Adler stated, reviewing his notes.

"And someone who implements creative problem solving to achieve fast results," Hester DeVries stated, also looking straight at Liv.

"Yes, that would also be very useful." Adler glanced up, staring straight at Liv. "Unfortunately, we don't have anyone who meets those criteria."

Clark cleared his throat. "I believe Councilor Ludwig and Councilor DeVries were referring to Liv. She was successful with the fae negotiations."

"If by successful, you mean that she helped a new leader to take over power from Queen Visa, then sure, I guess," Adler stated.

"A fae she has personal dealings with, and asked to attend his coronation," Raina corrected.

"I don't think that's relevant to this current case," Bianca said.

"That's the first time a Royal has been invited to a fae's coronation," Hester said, leaning forward to talk to Raina.

"I was there as well," Emilio stated proudly.

"As Warrior Beaufont's guest," Hester corrected.

"And you've already botched up the elf negotiations, Mr. Mantovani," Adler added.

"I wasn't asking for that case," Emilio said. "Actually, I wanted to say—"

"That you're ready to take your leave, having already been assigned your case," Bianca cut in.

Emilio's scowl deepened. "No, speaking of the fae—"

"We're actually discussing the elves," Adler interrupted. "And your sister is correct. Why are you still here?"

Letting out a breath, Emilio deflated. "Yes, I'll just be leaving."

After he'd left the chamber, Adler glanced around like he was trying to decide where they'd left off. "Now, I think we only have one option left for the elves, and unfortunately it's you, Mr. Ludwig."

Having been off in thought, Stefan glanced up. "Me? Really? I get a different case?"

Adler sighed. "I don't see what choice we have. Try to remember that the elves pride themselves on their intellect, so if you can manage to string together coherent sentences, that will help."

Stefan bowed. "Me will do my bestest, but I ain't as learned as you."

Liv suppressed a grin. She had to give Stefan credit. He was every bit as much of a smartass as she was.

Adler rolled his eyes. "Just get the agreement signed. We can't have any more delays. The information will be sent to your codex."

"Do not worry, Councilor," Stefan said proudly. "I'll

report back to you with successful results as soon as possible."

"Although I highly doubt that," Adler began, "I most likely won't be here when you return."

This was apparently news to the council, causing many of them to stir.

"It's true," Adler said, cutting through the noise. "I've soon got to take leave to attend to personal matters."

"Are you getting married?" Liv dared to ask.

The crow known as Diabolos swooped down from above. Okay, so apparently it was a lie that Liv thought Adler was getting married. Sue her. Everyone could deduce that he wouldn't be a good lover, based on his sour attitude.

"What I'm doing is none of your business, Ms. Beaufont," Adler stated. "And the reason you were not assigned the elf case, as my peers seemed to be pushing for, is that you are now receiving your orders from Father Time. Isn't that correct?"

"I call him Papa, but yeah, I guess so," Liv stated. "At least for the time being."

"Does he have a case for you?" Adler asked, a strange curiosity in his voice.

Liv shrugged. "Yeah, he wanted me to do something with this chicken."

Adler blinked impatiently at her. "We don't have time for your antics. Does Father Time have a case for you?"

"Okay, since the truth isn't working for you," Liv stated. "Yes, Papa wants me to fix all the clocks in the Underground. Apparently, they are all off by two and a half minutes."

Diabolos cawed loudly at her, telling the council she was lying. But at least they knew she had been telling the truth before.

"And will you be meeting with Father Time on this case?" Adler questioned.

"I'm not sure it's our business," Hester dared to say. "Father Time supersedes our jurisdiction. If he has a case for one of our Warriors, then we have nothing further to say on the matter."

"I think the fact that she's our Warrior means we have every right to know what is going on," Adler said through gritted teeth. "We should be the ones signing off on this."

Liv elbowed Stefan in the side. "And here I thought it was my body, my case, and my rights."

He shook his head. "Shows how much you know. You're owned."

"Mr. Ludwig, what are you still doing here?" Adler questioned. "You've been assigned your case."

"Yes, but I have to wait for Liv," he answered.

"Because?" Bianca asked, staring down at him expectantly.

"Would you believe that she parked next to me but a bit too close and now I can't get into my car? I need her to move so I can get out."

Diabolos squawked at Stefan. In response, he simply smiled at the crow.

Shaking off his tomfoolery, Adler directed his attention back to Liv. "Will you be meeting with Father Time on this case?"

"Yeah, I guess so," Liv stated.

"And where do you meet with him?" Adler asked.

Liv narrowed her eyes at him. "I'm not at liberty to say."

He threw himself backward, a loud sigh falling from his mouth. "Well, how long will you be detained on this case?"

"Depends on the chicken," Liv answered.

Lorenzo stroked his black goatee. "I agree with your frustration on this matter, Adler. It is very disconcerting that the Father of Time has returned and taken ownership of one of ours, and we have no information on the matter."

"Again, I'm not owned by anyone," Liv cut in. "I'm a free agent."

"You are a Warrior for the House of Seven, and therefore answer to the council," Adler nearly yelled, his face flushing.

"She is," Clark stated confidently. "And for doing her job, she's been promoted in a way, earning the trust of the king of the fae, the giants, and Father Time."

"That's right," Raina said. "It seems you are more than sufficiently doing your job. Whatever Father Time assigns you, I'm certain you will carry out seamlessly."

Hester nodded. "When Father Time is done with you, please return to us. I'm sure we will have cases that could use your expertise."

Adler looked back and forth between the Councilors, but, having no way to argue, he simply bowed his head. "Yes, very well. You're dismissed."

CHAPTER SIX

"You said I boxed you in," Liv said, tapping her foot. She and Stefan stood on the boardwalk in front of the House of Seven, tourists strolling by and the Pacific Ocean lapping the shore in the distance.

He shrugged, suddenly looking quite boyish. "I was going to say we carpooled, but that might bring up all sorts of questions."

"Like, why are two magicians who have portal magic driving around the congested city of Los Angeles?"

He shook his head. "Nope, that's not what I thought the council would be thinking."

Liv realized what he had meant. "Right. Yeah, thanks for avoiding unnecessary rumors."

The beach bums pushing shopping carts and pale tourists snapping pictures swerved around the pair. Liv sensed Stefan wanted to say something, but for some reason he appeared reluctant, his eyes sliding to the restaurants and shops in the distance.

"Mommy!" a boy with a back-facing cap yelled. "I want

to get my palm read!" He pointed at the shop that was the entrance for the House of Seven.

"It's a scam, Billy," Liv imparted.

"My name is Kyle!" the boy blurted.

"Well, excuse me. *I'm* not a psychic," Liv said.

The mother, a round woman with rosy cheeks and a beehive hairdo, grabbed the kid by the hand and tugged him down the boardwalk. "What have I told you about talking to strangers?"

"She talked to me!" the kid yelled.

"Did you see what they were wearing?" the woman said to her husband, looking over her shoulder at Liv and Stefan, who was wearing all black like her.

"They must be goths or devil worshippers," the husband said, putting a protective arm around his wife's shoulder.

Liv sighed. "We risk our lives every single day so they can get fat on McDonald's." She waved at the family, who was still gawking over their shoulders as they waddled away. "You're welcome."

Stefan laughed. "I sort of like the negative judgments. They light a fire under my ass."

"You sure it isn't the remnants of demon blood in your system?" Liv teased.

"Well, there is that, too." Stefan pointed to the nearest pub. "You want to grab a drink real fast?"

"Actually, what I'd like to do is spend the rest of the afternoon in that place and stumble home to my bed," Liv stated. "I haven't had a night off in...well, I can't remember."

"I believe your last night off, you insisted on helping me demon-hunt in France."

"That was sort of like a vacation," Liv argued.

"Until the vampire attacked," Stefan added.

"True, true," Liv replied. "And I'll have to take a raincheck on the drink. I've got to go pick up my chicken."

Stefan rocked back on his heels, looking at the clear blue sky. "Of course you were serious about that."

"Of course, I was. Diabolos didn't call me out on it," Liv stated. "Which makes me wonder if there isn't some way to get around that ward since we know that Adler is a skinny little liar. Bianca too, for that matter. And who knows who else?"

"Oh, and here I thought you and Bianca were besties," Stefan teased.

"We braid each other's hair at night," Liv joked. "And what do you think is going on with her and Emilio?"

He shrugged. "Something suspect, but knowing those two, it's nothing of consequence. They aren't people who have real problems. Just socialites who need to run other people down to feel better about themselves."

"Why don't you tell me how you really feel about them."

"So this chicken?" Stefan asked.

"It's apparently a person. A smart one who draws mathematical equations in the dirt," Liv explained.

"How in the world do you find such characters?"

"They're attracted to my brand of crazy," Liv answered.

"I guess we should start a club, then."

Liv pretended to be interested in the homeless man digging through the trash. "So, you got your wish."

"No, I didn't, because we're not having a drink right now. I still owe you one for saving my life."

"And you think a drink will be sufficient payment?" she teased.

"It's a start," he retorted.

She shook her head. "You got a different case."

Stefan sighed. "Yeah, but I got the impossible one that everyone's failed at."

Liv threw up her hands. "I thought you said you wanted to use your brains." She tilted her head, a curious glare in her eyes. "That was a lie, wasn't it? You don't *have* any brains, do you?"

He laughed. "I'll admit that I'm mostly muscle and sweet moves, but I know a thing or two."

"Then figure out where the others have failed with the elf negotiations and use a different strategy," Liv offered. "I'm not sure I even understand what's such a big deal with this elf business."

Stefan gawked at her before recovering. "Oh, I forget that you've been away for a while. Well, the elves have threatened to stop obeying the rule of the House of Seven."

"Was that *before* Decar killed a bunch of them?" Liv guessed.

Stefan nodded. "Yeah, he apparently thought brutality would change their minds."

"But it didn't."

"No, and if they refuse our rule, then others will do the same, in effect making us useless," Stefan explained.

Even though others didn't know the truth about the House of Fourteen, Liv believed they sensed it. The House was losing its reputation because it didn't have its balance, and the elves knew it. Still, she didn't want to lose her job. Instead, she wanted to fix the organization. "What if…" Liv began slowly. "What if you invited them to have a seat on the council?"

The laugh that spilled from Stefan's mouth made a group of tourists turn around. "Adler would never go for that. Not just him, but the others. The House is made up of Royals. That's the way it has always been. A random elf diplomat can't sit on the council. Then all the other races would want a seat, and it would be a chaotic mess."

Which was why it used to be mortals and magicians. That made so much sense now. The two largest races ruling over the magical world. One with a vested interest in magic, and the other with an interest in the world at large.

"Yeah, that makes sense," Liv stated. "But they are echoing my own concerns."

"Which is why you should be the one working this case," Stefan said. "You'd put on some green tights and waltz in there offering them something they couldn't refuse."

"Hey, why can't you wear tights?" Liv asked with mock seriousness.

"I'm not really the Peter Pan type," he remarked.

"Well, I'd go on the case with you, but there's that whole Father Time being my boss thing."

He waved her off. "Yeah, yeah. Same old, same old. It's all excuses with you."

Something suddenly occurred to Liv, and she wasn't sure why she hadn't wondered it before. "Why is it that the Royals in the House are currently all brothers and sisters? My parents were Councilor and Warrior, but that was because my father was an only child and his parents were ready to step down when he married my mother."

Stefan thought for a moment. "I guess it's just a fluke. If Raina got married, for instance, and I wanted to step down, her husband could take my place. She's the eldest, so the Councilor gets to make these decisions."

"Oh, then I guess it's based on the age range and social habits of the current Royals," Liv jested. "Mostly young'uns in the Seven right now are socially awkward and not interested in coupling up."

"Yes, mostly," Stefan said with an air of mystery.

Liv took a step backward, her chest suddenly buzzing with a strange energy, almost like the one she felt before a battle. However, this one was different. Better, somehow. "I better get going. I don't want to keep the chicken waiting. Good luck with the elves."

"Thanks, but I'll need more than luck. Maybe loan me some of that Liv Beaufont charm."

She shook her head. "You've got your own. I'm sure of it. Just don't treat them like they're demons or we'll be in trouble."

"I promise, I'm no Decar Sinclair," Stefan said.

Liv halted. "I know. That's why I like you. You're not a scoundrel. At least as far as I can tell."

"I promise I'm not," Stefan said, a meaningful look in his eyes. "But you can maybe decide when I buy you that drink."

"Yeah, maybe…" Liv said, continuing to step away from the dark figure giving her a piercing stare, his blue eyes like freshly polished sapphires.

CHAPTER SEVEN

The Santa Ana winds picked up, scattering leaves across the street as Liv neared Rory's house.

"You know he's following you," Plato said by her side, not having said a word since joining her after the portal.

She halted, her hands on her hips. "Seriously? I thought I'd spoken to Stefan about that."

Plato shook his head. "Sorry, I should have been more specific. I forgot you have multiple men with stalker issues."

"What? It's not Stefan? Who is it?" Liv asked.

"Adler," Plato said in a whisper.

Liv slipped behind the closest tree, looking over her shoulder. "Are you serious? Since when did he take it upon himself to trail me?"

"Since now," Plato answered.

"Thanks for all your immense help," Liv said, suddenly feeling breathless. "But still. I get that he's suspicious of me, but why follow me now? Why not before?"

"Before you were a pest," Plato reasoned. "Now you

work for Father Time and one of the mortal Seven and have recovered your mother's sword, and then there's that whole going into the ancient chamber thing. But those are all wild guesses."

Liv shook her head. "He doesn't know about all that. Well, unless he just heard you talking to me."

"Has anyone ever overhead us?" Plato asked.

"I don't know. All I'm certain of is that you disappear when someone comes around," Liv stated.

"Correct, which means he's far enough away that you're safe for now," Plato stated. "He doesn't want to catch you. Probably only follow you."

Liv nodded. "Okay, well, but I'm headed to Rory's now."

"Which is fine, because it's now common knowledge that you and the giant are friends," Plato stated. "He was your date for the coronation, after all."

"Ewe," Liv said. "He was invited by King Butthead."

"Right," Plato chirped. "Liv isn't attracted to giants."

"Why are you talking about me in the third person?"

"I'm trying it out."

"It doesn't work," she replied.

"What *is* your type?"

"I don't have one," Liv answered.

"Now, now, no man is an island," Plato stated.

"Would you focus for a moment?" Liv implored. "I've got to figure out what to do with Councilor Uptightness."

"Well, continue to Rory's house and get your chicken. Then take three portals to Roya Lane," Plato ordered, becoming a very authoritative presence suddenly.

"But what if he…"

"Leave Adler to me," Plato stated. "I'll serve as a diversion when he tries to follow you after you leave here."

"How will you do that?" Liv asked

He simply offered her a look that plainly said, "You know I'm not going to tell you that."

"Okay, thanks," Liv said. "You're the cat's meow."

He lowered his head, shaking it.

Liv laughed, continuing on to Rory's.

When Liv approached Rory's door, it swung back, just as she expected. It actually made her feel comforted to know that he was home and things were normal. At least they were here.

However, when she stepped through the door, the sight before her was anything but normal.

"Ummm…are you having a candlelit dinner with a chicken?" she asked, taking in the scene of Rory sitting on one side of his dining room table, a napkin tucked into his shirt collar. On the other side of the table, sitting on a stack of books was the chicken. Spread between them were several dishes, and in the center was a set of candles.

"She's not a chicken. She's a person, and I'm trying to make her feel comfortable," Rory explained.

"Currently, she's a chicken, but I appreciate your thoughtful approach." Liv whistled, taking in the many dishes on the table. Their yummy aromas floated through the air. "Do I have to be turned into livestock to get such a fancy spread?"

"I'm trying to figure out what Dorothy likes to eat,"

Rory said, raising an eyebrow at the bird. It squawked twice.

"Dorothy?" Liv questioned.

He shook his head. "That's not her name, but I keep trying. I've been through Debra, Angela, Rebecca, and Monica. Those are it."

"I'm not sure the chicken's name is really what's important here," Liv said. "But it's sweet that you're trying to make her comfortable." She waved the smell from the closest dish up to her face. "Is this chicken makhani? You know that's my favorite, right?"

"I do now," Rory stated.

"Wait, but you're offering chicken to a chicken? You do get the insensitivity here, right?" Liv asked.

"She isn't a chicken, though," Rory said. "She's a person, and she hasn't liked any of the regular chicken feed I've offered her. So I tried something a bit more international."

Liv glanced around the table, noticing the Thai curry, enchiladas, pizza, and Korean barbeque. "Right. This isn't strange at all. You've made an international buffet of food for a chicken."

"A person," Rory corrected.

"Still, we need to get you out more," Liv said, thinking of the giant lady they'd met in Texas. Matilda.

"So you've come for Jennifer?" Rory asked, glancing sideways at the chicken.

She squawked twice.

Liv shook her head. "No, I don't think she was born in middle America in the nineteen eighties. Let's keep trying, though. Guess the chicken's name game is super fun. And yes, I'm going to take her to Father Time. He wants me to do something or another. It will be convoluted and strange and I'll probably die in the process, but don't you worry your pretty head about me."

Rory was busy putting different things into a bag and didn't appear worried in the least.

"Are you packing me a lunch?" Liv asked. "I did forget to eat. That's mighty thoughtful of you."

"I'm packing up stuff for Maggie," Rory said, glancing at the chicken.

Another two squawks.

"Oh, right. How strange of me to think you were worried about my wellbeing," Liv stated. "And by the way, Adler Sinclair followed me here."

Rory's head shot up, horror in his gaze. "*The* Adler Sinclair?"

Liv shook her head. "There's only one. But don't worry, Plato is taking care of him."

"Don't worry?" Rory questioned, moving even faster to pack things up. "If he followed you, then he's—"

"On to me," Liv said, finishing his sentence. "It could be. Or it could be this Father Time business. He doesn't like being left out of the mix. Anyway, don't worry. Plato will draw him away from your house and get him off my trail. You have nothing to worry about. I'd never put you in danger."

Rory nodded. "I know. I'm just so worried, with Mum being out there working on leads and you working with Father Time. And it's my busy season, or else I'd do more."

"Busy season?" Liv asked. "Like in the grocery business?"

He shook his head. "I'm not telling you what I do for a living. And groceries? You think I run a store?"

Liv shrugged. "You're good with produce. I don't know."

Rory handed her the bag of assorted foods he'd packed. Then he picked up the chicken, hugging it lightly before handing it to her. "Be careful with her. She likes to be carried under one arm, and she goes to bed at around ten o'clock. She takes her coffee straight, and usually naps for a half hour after lunch."

Liv shook her head at him. "You're a very strange giant, Rory."

He blushed, realizing how much he'd obsessed over this chicken lady.

Liv, catching the embarrassment on his face, smiled at him. "And you know what? I wouldn't have you any other way. Stay strange."

CHAPTER EIGHT

I f Liv thought she got a lot of curious glances before
   when she was on Roya Lane, they were now doubled.
Usually, passersby avoided her gaze and hid from her,
afraid she was going to break up their gambling businesses
or stop them from selling illegal magical tech. Today they
gawked at her for too long, many of them poking their
companions in the arm and pointing directly at her.

"Pointing is rude," Liv fired at a fairy who was giggling
with her friend, the two hovering a few feet off the cobble-
stone road as they picked out dragon fruit. It wasn't the
stuff they sold at mortals' grocery stores. This stuff actually
got hot when it was ripe, burst into flames, and then
opened into a beautiful, delectable flower that could be
enjoyed once it had cooled.

The fairies turned their backs on Liv as she passed, but
were soon staring at her again over their shoulders.

"Haven't you ever seen a chicken before?" Liv asked a
gnome who had let his marmalade ice cream drop into his
lap, so engrossed was he with watching her pass.

If the patrons on Roya Lane gawked at her for carrying a chicken, Liv could only wonder what would happen if she was in Los Angeles, walking down the boardwalk on the beach. Actually, things were so weird in that city, they might not pay her any notice. She could just tell people the chicken was her emotional comfort animal. Maybe get it a vest that made it look legitimate.

"They are all a bunch of freaks," Liv said to the chicken in a hushed voice, scanning the street as eccentric magicians and dirty elves passed her, staring. "However, they see a Warrior carrying a chicken, what I now realize looks like a diaper bag, and two swords, and they think they are all of a sudden normal."

The chicken gobbled quietly as if she knew to keep her voice down. Wouldn't want to draw any more attention.

Thankfully, the crowd thinned when Liv reached the end of the lane. To her surprise, Subner the gnome's shop had its doors wide open. The windows had been cleaned, and sparkling and fancy merchandise was displayed on velvet fabrics. The sign over the awning read The Fantastical Armory.

Liv poked her head through the door, to find even more changes. The carpet had been cleaned, and all of the cases dusted. Overhead, the chandelier gave off a shimmering light, making the mirrors on the wall dazzle. The only thing that detracted from the shop's pristine appearance was that almost all of the cases were empty.

Sitting behind the countertop, Subner glanced up from his crossword puzzle. "There you are! Papa Creola said to expect you."

Liv set the chicken down on a counter and dropped the

bag on the floor. "Yes, Papa Creola apparently has a case for me involving this chicken. I'm here for my orders."

Subner slid off the stool and came around the counter, eyeing the bird with disdain. "That creature better not drop anything. I just cleaned that case."

"Don't worry, she's trained," Liv said. "I think…"

"Papa Creola isn't here," Subner said, a scowl on his face as he glared up at the chicken, who was pecking at the glass.

"Well, he really should be better at managing his calendar, because he told me to stop by at this time to see him."

Subner rolled his eyes at her. "Yes, he was aware that you'd be coming by. He has other business, and asked that you help me with something."

"Does it involve this chicken named Gloria?" Liv asked, an inflection on the last word.

The chicken squawked twice.

"Yeah, yeah, you're not a Gloria. Got it," Liv retorted to the bird.

"No, it doesn't. The chicken is your responsibility until you can meet with Papa Creola, but he was adamant that you keep her safe. It's absolutely crucial," Subner explained.

"When he was referring to the bird, did he use a name?" Liv asked.

"No, he did not," Subner said at once. "Now, do you still have the sword that I modified for you?"

Liv pulled back her cloak on one side to show Bellator. "I never leave home without it."

Subner nodded. "Very good. As you can see, my weapons store is lacking inventory. I was hoping you'd help me with that."

"Right…" Liv said, drawing out the last word. "Because I was looking for more side jobs."

"Well, it's under Papa Creola's orders, and I believe you report to him directly," Subner explained, his hands behind his back as he rocked forward on his toes, looking important.

"I do report to him directly…when he's here," Liv jested.

"And also, I believe you were going to ask a favor of me, weren't you?" Subner asked, a sly grin on his face.

Liv's hand reached for Inexorabilis. The sword was on her other hip, that familiar small zap of electricity running through her fingers as they met the metal. "How did you know about that?"

He actually smirked, which might have been a first for Liv to see. "My boss can see the future."

"*Our* boss," Liv corrected. "And yes, I do need your help with something."

"Then we have mutual interests and reasons to help each other, it seems."

Liv sighed. She needed Subner's help with her mother's sword. Side missions were time-consuming, but this one could be worth it if she got the gnome's help. "Fine. What do you want me to do for you? If it involves goats, cows, or horses, I'm out."

He shook his head. "It doesn't. What I need is for you to recover an arsenal of weapons that was stolen from me long ago."

This was par for the course, Liv thought. "Okay, fine. Where can I find them, and what sort of beasts do I have to battle?"

"I have no idea, and I'm sure it will be something lethal."

Trying to keep her cool, she rolled her head around. "How do you want me to find these weapons if you can't tell me where to look?"

He shrugged. "If I knew where to look, I would have recovered them long ago. All I can tell you is that they are probably hidden, and Bellator will help you unlock wherever they are locked up."

"That's all you can tell me?" Liv asked dryly.

"Oh, and one other thing," Subner said, throwing a single finger in the air. "They were referred to as Dequiem set. There's nothing like them in the world. They are all gnome-made, imbued with special magic, and incredibly valuable. If I have those in my shop, it will give it the reputation I need to compete with the other stores on the Lane."

"Crazy thought," Liv began. "Couldn't you just advertise that this is Father Time's store? He's pretty much got the most cred on the streets, from what I've heard. Well, besides not being able to keep appointments."

Subner sighed, heat flaring in his eyes. "This is *my* shop. It always has been. But when Father Time went into hiding, I offered it to him as a sanctuary. It will continue to be his main office, but I want my new shop to have its own reputation separate from Papa."

"Okay, fine," Liv said, holding up her hands, sensing the little guy's anger rising. "So you need me to find the Dequiem set, but you don't know where I should look. How many swords and whatnots are we talking about?"

"Fifty," Subner answered at once.

Liv's mouth fell open. "I had enough trouble carrying two swords and a chicken down Roya Lane. How do you expect me to return fifty swords from an unknown location to you?"

Subner held out his hand, and a green bag made of crushed velvet appeared. "That I actually have a solution for. Everything will fit into this."

Liv lifted the bag and peered into it, not believing that fifty swords could fit into the small pouch. "Let me guess, it is bigger on the inside?"

"Something like that," he answered.

"Okay, so I'll go on your impossible mission, but will you at least keep the chicken for me?" Liv asked.

He shook his head at once. "I can't. Papa Creola explicitly said you were to take her."

Liv gritted her teeth, making eye contact with the chicken. "How am I supposed to recover these weapons while carrying a chicken about? Can I put her in the bag?"

"Not if you want to keep her alive," Subner answered.

"Fine," Liv said with a sigh. "Any other impossible factors you want to add to this mission? Maybe require that I do it blindfolded, or while balancing a book on my head?"

"That would be ridiculous," Subner stated, snapping his fingers at her. "Let me see this sword you've brought."

Liv thought the gnome's cantankerous manner was sort of endearing, like an old hound dog who didn't much care for the spritely puppies born in the spring. She withdrew Inexorabilis from its sheath, offering it to Subner.

His eyes widened at the sight of the blade. "You've recovered Guinevere Beaufont's sword."

"Wait, did Papa Creola tell you what I was bringing you?"

He shook his head, studying the sword. "Only that you'd need help with a weapon."

"Yes, and my mother locked a memory into the sword. At least, that's the impression I get."

Subner nodded, his blue eyes studying every inch of the blade. "Your assumption is correct. It feels like a full vault."

"Can you access the information?" she asked hopefully.

"Oh, no," he answered at once. "Only the maker can."

Liv deflated. "I heard my mother's voice when I picked up the sword. She said, 'I have buried memories deep within this sword, and only an expert can uncover them.'"

"Although I'm most adept at weaponry, I can't help you with this sword," Subner explained. "Only the elf who made it will be able to unlock the messages."

"Can you help me with finding that person?"

"I'm not certain who it was, but I can try," Subner said, laying the sword down on the countertop next to the chicken, who was eyeing the blade with her head tilted to the side. "You'll have to leave the sword with me, though."

Liv hesitated, her chest tightening. She'd only just gotten the blade back, and she couldn't fathom something happening to it and breaking her promise to Sophia. But she needed Subner's help.

"If I do, then—"

"Nothing will happen to your mother's sword," he interrupted her. "I will guard it with my life. But I'll need to study the weapon to determine exactly who made it. Then I can tell who they are, and possibly how to find them."

Liv pushed out a breath, breaking up the tension in her chest. "Very well, then. I look forward to finding out what you discover."

"Once you return with the Dequiem set," Subner said, kneeling and picking up the bag of provisions for the chicken like he was trying to encourage her to leave.

"Okay, I sense you're not changing your mind about keeping Cindy, then," Liv said.

The chicken squawked twice.

Subner shook his head. "I wish you well on your travels, Warrior Beaufont."

"Thanks," Liv said, sticking the chicken under one arm. "I'm going to need it."

CHAPTER NINE

Holding the chicken and a bag of assorted foods and staring at the hustle and bustle of Roya Lane, Liv tried to figure out her options. She needed to find the Dequiem set, but she had no idea where to look. Considering her resources, she tried to determine what the best way to solve this problem would be. There was always a solution at her disposal, and all she had to do was find it.

Liv half expected to see Rudolf doing something ridiculous as she continued down the Lane. However, he was king of the fae now, and probably—hopefully—had better things to do. She halted in front of a brick wall and suddenly realized that she was the ridiculous one now, carrying a chicken and its day bag.

How had things gotten to this point, she wondered, stepping up close to the entrance for the brownie's official headquarters. Liv didn't know if Mortimer would know anything about the weapons, but he was her best hope. If nothing else, he might be able to offer her a clue.

She announced her presence to the solid brick wall,

waiting for the doorway to materialize the way it usually did. When it didn't, she cleared her throat.

"Ummm…Mortimer?" Liv began. "It's me, Liv Beaufont, Warrior for the House of Seven. Are you home?"

Somehow things had gotten even weirder. Liv was holding a chicken and talking to herself, making even more people gawk at her.

"Seriously, where are you, Mortimer?" Liv asked, refraining from kicking the wall.

The chicken bawked, flapping her wing to release herself from Liv's grasp. Feathers rained down as Liv let the bird go, stepping back when she continued to flap until she was settled on the road.

Liv wasn't sure what had gotten into the bird, who was pecking the brick in a rhythmic motion, as if putting in a code.

"Ummm…what are you doing, Ava?" Liv asked.

The chicken squawked twice, continuing to peck at different bricks. Up, down, up, down, left, right, left, right. It was too much of a pattern to be a fluke, Liv thought.

And then suddenly the door to the Brownie's office materialized.

The chicken stepped back, looking at Liv with an impassive expression.

Liv pointed at the door and then the chicken. "Did you just do that?"

One squawk. A yes.

Liv eyed the bird and then the door. "You're very strange."

Pricilla wasn't at her desk when they entered the office. The reception area and hallway were still clean and organized, as they had been the last time Liv was there. "I'd tell you to wait here," Liv said to the chicken in her arms, "but I'm under strict orders to keep you safe, so it looks like we're best buds for a while."

As they neared Mortimer's office door, a series of giggles could be heard. Liv covered her mouth when a more intimate sound emanated from the other side of the door. She was about to turn around and run for the exit when the chicken squawked loudly. Liv's eyes widened in horror as she covered the bird's beak.

Before she could run, Mortimer opened the door a crack and peered through. "Who…oh, Warrior Beaufont. What a pleasant surprise."

"I'm sorry, is this a bad time?" Liv asked in a rush. "We didn't mean to sneak in. It's just that my chicken…well, she isn't really mine. I don't know who she belongs to. Maybe to herself. Anyway, she opened the door, and I let myself in because I need your help."

Mortimer kept looking to the side, seemingly distracted by whoever was on the other side of the door. Pressing down his disorderly hair, the brownie opened the door. "No, this is a perfect time. We just couldn't hear you knock, we were so busy working in here."

Pricilla, his new receptionist, appeared beside him, her tight skirt bunched up and her blouse buttoned wrong. "Yes, I was helping with filing, but we're all done here."

"Filing…" Liv said, looking around the office. It wasn't full of papers like it had been before, and the walls weren't lined with filing cabinets. Actually, there was only Mortimer's desk, a computer, and the picture window.

There was a giggle from Pricilla just before Mortimer closed the door. "Please take a seat, Liv Beaufont. I'm happy to see you today."

Mortimer, in fact, looked happier than Liv had ever seen him. He had also dropped a bit more weight and was looking even sharper than usual.

"So, you and Pricilla," Liv said, letting the statement hang in the air.

"Yes, she's a fine assistant," Mortimer said, blushing as he took his seat.

"I see that," Liv said, hiding a grin.

He leaned across the desk. "I'm not sure if I should be telling you this, but I think of you as a friend."

"Of course," Liv replied. "I think of you the same way."

"Well, it's sort of a secret, but Pricilla and I are dating."

"No?" Liv said, mock surprise in her voice.

He nodded proudly. "It's true. And all because of you."

"Me?"

"Yes! You pushed me to get an assistant and encouraged me to get outside myself. And many of the cases you've brought to me have reminded me that I'm not getting any younger. One day, I just decided I'd take the risk and ask her out. And guess what she said?"

"Yes?"

Again he nodded. "Can you believe it? I think she really likes me."

"Well, you *are* quite the catch," Liv gushed.

He blushed even more. "So, what can I do for you today? Please excuse the mess in here. Local 420 is currently on strike for better wages, and it's really gotten me behind on things."

Liv glanced around the spotless office. "Ummm...I couldn't tell. And Local 420?"

"Yes, the Food and Commercial Workers Union," Mortimer explained, tossing his head from shoulder to shoulder. "Every few decades, one of the unions acts up, asking for something. I guess I was overdue for this."

Liv set the chicken on the floor, again hoping she was potty trained. She didn't want her messing up Mortimer's pristine office. "Well, I hope the union stuff gets sorted out."

"It will eventually," Mortimer said with a smile. "Now, what does Liv Beaufont, Warrior for the House of Seven, want today?"

"Well, I know this is a long shot, but I'm looking for a set of weapons by the name of Dequiem. It's roughly fifty swords that went missing. Can you ask around and have your brownies keep an eye out?"

"I can do one better." Mortimer began typing wildly on his keyboard. "I've upgraded our systems so that we inventory and catalog items of interest. For one, it makes cleaning assignments easier, and secondly, I figured it might be of help to you."

"Wow, thank you," Liv said, impressed. "You've come a long way from your paper system, haven't you?"

"Don't even remind me that I used to be so archaic," Mortimer said. "It's a wonder I ever got anything done."

"I'm sure you're enjoying the efficiency."

"Well, I'll be taking my first vacation in a few hundred years, so I'd say," Mortimer shared.

"That's great!" Liv exclaimed. "Where are you going?"

"Disney World," Mortimer answered. "Pricilla has always wanted to do the teacup ride."

"Are you two tall enough for that one?" Liv asked, then shook her head. "Never mind. I'm sure you'll figure it out."

He nodded, squinting at the computer. "Yes, it appears that one of my brownies inventoried something they listed as the Dequiem consisting of at least fifty gnome-made swords."

"Yes, that's it!" Liv yelped. "Where are they?"

The light expression on Mortimer's face dropped. "Not a place that most magicians can easily enter, even with your magic. You'll need one of my brownies to get past the locks.'"

"Actually, I had some modifications made to my sword. Maybe the locks aren't a problem," Liv stated. "Where are the weapons?"

"They are located in a secret chamber inside the Tabularium in the Forum in Rome," Mortimer answered.

"That sounds complicated," Liv stated.

He nodded. "Yes. It's a confusing mass of old buildings and ancient ruins. Even knowing where the weapons are won't make locating them easy."

"I kind of figured that," Liv joked.

"Now, I have one of my best located there. If you run into problems, he should be able to help."

"Thanks," Liv said. "Is there anything else you can tell me to narrow the search?"

Mortimer studied his screen for a moment. "It appears the weapons are heavily guarded. Be prepared for a fight, but do try to be careful not to damage the structure. It is necessary to preserve it for historical purposes."

"Got it," Liv stated. "Fight the beasts, recover the weapons, and don't torch the ancient runes in Rome. That's a regular Wednesday afternoon for me."

CHAPTER TEN

For some reason, Liv was unable to portal directly into the Forum in Rome. It probably had to do with wards set up centuries before by Romans trying to protect their city from foreign magicians or other magical creatures. However, as Liv stared at the line to get into the Forum, it was a sick joke.

"How am I supposed to get in there?" Liv asked, mostly to herself.

The chicken, who apparently had an opinion on everything, squawked.

"Yes, and the other question is, how am I going to sneak you in there?" Liv grumbled. "I don't suppose I can drop you off at that café across the way and pick you up later, huh?"

Squawk.

Liv nodded, pretending she understood the complaint. "Yes, I am to keep you safe at all costs. I remember."

Placing a glamour on the chicken, Liv made her appear to be a toddler in her arms. She would have done that before, but it was a drain on her magic—which meant she needed to get through the security line fast.

Turning to gauge the line into the Forum, Liv caught the sight of the Coliseum in the distance. It was hard to believe these structures had been standing for so long. Their history, or at least the history that had been recorded, was barbaric and strange. And yet, the Romans had preserved them, honoring their past, unlike the magicians, who had covered up the great war, brainwashing those who had lost and even those who had won.

"I'm guessing it's unlikely that one of these bazillion tourists will allow me to cut in line if I tell them I'm on official business for Father Time," Liv said in a hushed voice to the chicken.

The chicken apparently had no opinion about that.

"Excuse me, miss," a guy with slicked-back hair and a leather jacket said in a thick Roman accent. "Do you have your tickets yet?"

"No," Liv said, looking around for a ticket office. She was going to complain bitterly to Subner about this. The weapons weren't just held in a place to which she couldn't portal, but she had to pay in order to get into the area. Liv considered magicking some tickets like she'd done when entering the National History Museum in Los Angeles. However, she was trying to be mindful of her magic use. She had no idea what she'd face to get to the Dequiem set.

"For forty euros, I can sell you a skip-the-line pass," the man said, leaning in entirely too close.

"That's not a bad deal for tickets," Liv said to the chicken, although she appeared to be a freckled little girl with pigtails.

"Oh, that's just for the skip the line. The tickets are twelve euros," the man corrected.

"So the pass to get past all these mouth-breathers is almost four times the actual cost of the ticket?" Liv asked skeptically.

"That's right," the man said.

"I'm not sure that's a good deal," Liv muttered.

"But this isn't the line to get the tickets. That's over there. You have to wait in line to get in, and there's also a separate line to get your tickets at the Coliseum. Then there's a line to actually get in."

"I don't think this math makes much sense."

"But if you get the skip-the-line pass, then I also have your ticket."

"Fine," Liv said, grateful when she pulled her money out and it automatically changed to euros. At least she hadn't had to exchange currency.

"Now, I'll just need another fifty-two euros for your beautiful daughter," the man said, continuing to hold out his hand.

Liv glared at the chicken. "Seriously? I have to pay for you as well? I really think I should have left you at a café."

The man gave her a startled look.

Realizing her mistake, Liv blushed. "She's a very mature toddler. Practically raising herself."

She pulled more money out of her pocket, depositing it into the man's hand as he gave her the tickets. "Okay, miss. Just get in this line for the Forum, and you'll be set."

"Wait," Liv stammered. "I thought you just sold me skip-the-line passes."

"I did," he said proudly. "That made it so you skipped

the line at the Coliseum to buy your tickets, but you still have to wait in the security line at the Forum."

"You Romans are tricky people," Liv grumbled.

He bowed slightly. "Yes, and I'm most grateful to have been of service to you."

Liv shook her head, going to the back of the line, which was even longer than before. Behind her, a group of tourists who had no idea what personal space was breathed on her shoulder, talking loudly.

While Liv was standing in the slow-moving line, at least a dozen more vultures came by, trying to sell her tickets and skip-the-line passes. She couldn't bring herself to ignore them, and instead simply muttered, "No, thanks. I've already been scammed once today."

When Liv was finally at the front of the security line, she realized she was going to have to remove her cape, Bellator, which looked like an umbrella, her belt, and all her other personal belongings from her pockets.

She set the chicken down so she could start the long process of removing her items.

"Miss!" A security guard ran over. "You can't put a child on the conveyor belt. She'll be x-rayed."

"Oh, right," Liv said, sort of overwhelmed by mortal security processes. She picked up the chicken and set her on the ground. "You can walk on your own, can't you, Michelle?"

The chicken squawked twice.

So not Michelle, Liv thought. Got it.

"Remove all your items," the guard said, pointing at the sheath on Liv's belt.

"Oh, hell. This is going to take forever." Liv immediately

regretted not using magic to get past all these security protocols. Thankfully, Bellator didn't set off any alarms when it passed through the machines.

Liv reasoned that she'd used less magical energy glamouring things than if she'd used magic to bypass this process. With her hands full, she worked to put her belt and sheath back on as the chicken clucked and pecked behind her, following.

"I guess we can call this a humbling experience," Liv said to the bird.

Once she had Bellator back into place and her cloak over her shoulders, Liv set off down the path snaking between the ancient ruins of the Forum.

"Mindy, if you look over here, you'll see a bunch of old columns," Liv said to the chicken, who clucked twice in response.

"That's a good question," Liv said, pretending she had understood. "The building was built last year, but due to acid rain, has fallen on hard times. It was a convenience mart that sold organic smoothies and selfie sticks to tourists."

The chicken clucked.

"Yes, you're probably right that they just call them smoothies in Italy since they don't pollute their food with chemicals like us Americans."

The chicken clucked twice loudly.

Liv gave her a startled expression as a group turned around to gawk. It probably sounded to them like the toddler she was carrying around was having a tantrum. "So you're not American? Is that what you're trying to tell me?"

One cluck.

"Okay, well, now we're making progress," Liv said, passing by the Arch of Titus. "I know your name isn't Mindy, Michelle, Dorothy, Jennifer, or Cindy and that you're not American. Wow, I'll crack this case in no time at this rate."

The chicken shook in her arms as if frustrated.

"Yes, that was sarcasm," Liv stated. "It's my first language. What's yours? Chinese? Japanese? Spanish? Oh, man, if you're not English, I've been trying all the wrong names, haven't I? Is your name Maria? Hana? Chun?"

The chicken squawked twice.

"Okay, well, I've got to focus on the task at hand right now, but later, I'll ask you more questions over a bottle of wine."

A man standing close by gave Liv a questioning look over his shoulder, obviously having overheard her.

She smirked at him. "Hey, a little wine is good for the child. Besides, when in Rome…"

Liv couldn't help herself. She laughed at her own joke as she marched past the Basilica di Santa Francesca Romana on her right.

"Seriously, I could really go for some pizza after we finish here," Liv stated. "You think you can hang out in a highchair and not make too much racket?"

The chicken clucked softly.

"We are making progress," Liv said. "Although I'm probably going to need my hands free soon. You good with being on the ground?"

The chicken clucked again.

Relieved, Liv set the chicken down. She turned in a complete circle, trying to get her bearings. "So, where is this Tabularium place? I guess I should have gotten a map from that jerk who scammed us with the tickets. I'm sure that would have only cost me another ten euros. Fifteen, if I wanted to skip the line to get the map, right?"

The chicken was busy scratching in the dirt as Liv took in the vastness of the Forum. She felt small as she stared up at the buildings that towered around her. High on a hill, the people who stood up there appeared like tiny ants.

"This place is pretty incredible, but also rather massive," Liv stated. "I don't know where to start looking."

The chicken squawked loudly.

Liv glanced down at the bird and realized she had sketched an arrow in the dirt, which pointed straight ahead.

"Oh, so you know your way, do you?"

A single cluck.

"Does that mean you're Italian?" Liv asked.

Another cluck.

"Well, looky there," Liv gushed. "I've figured you out." The light expression on her face dropped. "Oh, no. You were one of those awful vultures who swooped down on tourists selling them skip-the-line passes?"

Two clucks.

"A tour guide for the Forum?"

Two clucks.

"Well, at least I've eliminated those options." Liv continued in the direction the arrow pointed and passed the Basilica Julia. When she was about to keep going, the chicken clucked loudly, scratching at the ground with her feet like a bull about to charge.

Liv halted, pointing at the building. "That's it? The Tabularium?"

One cluck.

"All right, it's show time," Liv said. She put her hand on Bellator and carefully approached the building.

CHAPTER ELEVEN

Liv was about to head for the entrance to the Tabularium when she felt a sharp tug on her belt. She glanced down to find Bellator glowing slightly. Deciding to pull out the weapon, she was nearly thrown off balance when the sword swung in her hands like a compass trying to point north.

The tip of the sword pointed at a solid wall of the old building. Giving the chicken a tentative stare, Liv shrugged.

"Does this seem right to you?" she asked the bird.

It looked uncertain.

Holding the sword up next to the part of the wall that almost seemed to be magnetized, Liv tried to understand what she was missing. Could there be a secret door? Giants could see past the glamours on such walls. Liv sort of wished Rory was there right then, although he would have probably been doting on the chicken and giving her shit for getting scammed.

Holding Bellator like a key, Liv pushed it into the stone wall, expecting it to meet the hard surface. Instead, the large sword transformed into a small dagger and slipped into the solid stone. Turning it to the left, Liv heard a click. She pushed, and a creaking sound emanated.

Giving the chicken an impressed look, Liv pulled Bellator from the lock, and it instantly went back to its normal form. "Did you know about this entrance, Italian?"

The chicken squawked twice.

"Well, if you don't mind, I'm going first," Liv stated. "Stay close, chicken, and try not to be a distraction."

It was hard to believe Liv was entering an ancient building with a chicken. These sorts of situations should have been second nature by now, but the peculiarity of her life never got old.

When she stepped through the seemingly solid wall, Liv was greeted by total darkness. Holding up her hand, she created a fireball, which she'd learned how to harness so that they were torches as well as weapons.

"I'm guessing this isn't a place they allow tourists," Liv whispered to the chicken when she stepped into the passageway.

In the distance, she heard a gentle dripping sound. The smell of moisture was strong in the air, with an undertone of waste. It reminded Liv of one of the many times she'd had a case involving hanging out in a sewer system. Early in her career as a Warrior, Adler had constantly assigned her what she called "shitty" cases involving sewer systems. Liv could now brag that she knew the tunnels under many major cities better than the streets of Los Angeles.

Using Bellator as a compass, Liv held it in front of her in one hand, the fireball in the other. It directed her to the right when the tunnel split. Then to the left, and then down some steps. A cold draft hit Liv as she descended farther into the darkness.

Checking to ensure the chicken was keeping pace, Liv turned around. Not only was the bird right on her heels, but she pecked her in the calf, creating a sharp pain.

"Ouch! What did you do that for?" Liv asked, scowling at the animal.

It opened its beak, but nothing came out. Instead, horror radiated in the bird's eyes as it peered at something on the other side of Liv.

She froze and tensed. Listened to the sharp hissing at her back. "There's a snake behind me, isn't there?"

The chicken nodded its head slightly.

"Is it big?" Liv asked in a whisper.

Another nod.

"Damn it," Liv breathed. "I freaking hate snakes." She had faced a lophos when she was tracking down the canisters of magic. Things hadn't gone that well with that snake. She hadn't defeated it as much as tucked tail and run like hell through a portal. Facing another serpent wasn't Liv's idea of fun, but she guessed this was the monster guarding the weapons.

The monster lashed out at her, his tongue nearly connecting with her face. She ducked, feeling like a fish in a small pond. Liv brought Bellator up, and then she got her first clear vision of the monster.

It was massive.

And gross.

And scaly.

And somehow completely beautiful. Liv had never seen an anaconda like the one she was staring at. It was scary and stunning. It was beyond her imagination. She instantly wanted to pet the creature, but she knew it was much more powerful than her and would probably not be okay with her advances.

It was strange, because she knew anacondas were from the Amazon, yet this beast was here. The creature, which was as big around as a tree trunk, swayed back and forth. Liv was pretty certain that was what they did just before they squished a person or whatever they did. She had limited experiences with anacondas…well, none really.

She threw the fireball in her hand at the monster, but it swiveled to the right just before it hit, avoiding the missile. Liv created another fireball just as the other one extinguished on a back wall, plunging her into darkness again. She couldn't swing Bellator and also hold a fireball. Choices.

The snake's tongue flicked out of its mouth as it rose upright, towering high above her. It didn't appear the least bit intimidated by the fire, making Liv think that it might not harm the beast. There was only one way to find out.

Rapidly, Liv fired the ball at the snake and immediately created another one. This time the fire connected, and as she suspected, it did nothing, simply dissipated like it had hit a bank of snow.

Well, that changes everything, Liv thought with sudden dread. The one weapon she had access to wasn't going to slow the beast down. What she needed was light, but as far as she could tell, the area was bare bones. Brick walls and stone floors.

The snake lunged at Liv and she dove to the side, rolling and losing her fireball. Her first thought was for the chicken. Quickly creating another fireball, Liv was relieved to see the chicken was unharmed. Not only that, but she seemed to be putting the snake in a trance as she moved her head to one side and then the other, repeating the movement again and again.

Liv had no idea what was going on or how much longer the chicken could keep it up. That was when she noticed the torch on the far wall behind the chicken. It was quite a distance, and if Liv's aim wasn't perfect, the chicken was going to be roasted. Still, it was the best option Liv could find.

She hurled the fireball past the serpent. It soared over the chicken and crashed into the torch, igniting it and filling the cavernous area with light. The chicken's squawk sounded more like a child screaming as it bounced into the air, away from the embers raining down from the torch. The trance was broken and the snake struck at the chicken, thankfully missing. The bird flapped its wings and avoided the next attack, too.

Liv swung Bellator around just as the snake rounded on her. Knowing that hesitating would cost her the battle, Liv brought her sword through the air in a clean, swift move-ment. The blade sliced through the anaconda just under the head in a deliberate movement, severing the giant head from its body. The head rolled as the rest of the snake went completely limp.

Letting out a massive breath, Liv ensured that the

chicken was safe. Her relief was short-lived as a rattling sound emanated behind her.

"Since you killed my pet, it looks like I'll have to kill yours."

CHAPTER TWELVE

Liv spun to face the voice, Bellator warming in her hands after the recent kill. She probably should have expected the mangled face that stared at her from a glowing archway. It was a magician. Her ability to pick up on the brands of magic she'd been honing told her that much. What it didn't tell her was what had caused the long scars across the man's face, or why he shook when he held up his hand to brush his long gray hair out of his face.

"I'm sorry for killing your pet, but it was trying to kill me," Liv said, assessing her options. She could send a fireball at the madman, but something told her that might not work since it hadn't on his snake. There was also a lot of space between her and him, and the chicken was unfortunately between them.

He shrugged. "It's fine. We weren't that close. Not like I was with his mother, but I killed her myself."

"After she gave you those scars," Liv guessed.

The magician took a step forward. "I'm going to guess

since you're a magician wielding fireball magic, that Subner sent you to get my weapons."

"I believe he said they were his," Liv told him, her eyes sliding to the side as she started forward to try to put herself between the magician and the chicken.

A long yawn escaped the man's mouth. "Subner doesn't understand how the law of possession works."

"It's supposed to be three-fourths of the law," Liv corrected.

The magician's face contorted oddly when he made to smile. "I see that you have a very nice sword. Only something giant-made, of the highest quality, could have killed De Soto so efficiently."

"De Soto?" Liv asked. "That was the name of the oversized snake? I was guessing he was a Wayne."

"I think that adding your sword to my collection would be very nice," the magician said, eyeing Bellator with a hungry expression.

"Thing is, I'm not looking to part with the sword at this time," Liv stated. "I came to get weapons, not to give them."

The magician's laughter sounded like loose rocks sifting through a grate. "My power comes from merely possessing the Dequiem set. You're foolish to think you can challenge me in my home."

"Yeah, I get that a lot," Liv stated, unleashing a fireball and throwing it at the magician. It wasn't even halfway toward him when he simply flipped his hand and the fireball fell to the ground, extinguishing at once. As she had thought, fire wasn't going to work on this guy.

He laughed again. "Fire isn't an enemy to me. I enjoy it,

actually, unlike water. De Soto, now, he enjoyed water, which was why we hardly ever got along."

Liv exchanged an uneasy glance with the chicken. If this magician thought it was weird that the chicken was pecking at the stone floor, he didn't show it. Liv tried not to pay the bird much notice, but it was hard to miss that she was sketching a round pattern on the floor.

Liv wasn't sure what she was doing, but she was going to buy them some time while she tried to figure it out.

"So these weapons give you power simply by possessing them?" she asked the man.

"Why, yes!" he boomed. "You've heard of the Great Cheverone?"

"I haven't actually," Liv said, taking a step backward, feeling the tug from Bellator. It wanted her to back up as Cheverone neared her. She wasn't sure why, since it usually lusted for a battle.

The magician laughed as if Liv were joking. "I'm known all over the world for my incredible powers. That incident that happened in Budapest with the fences? That was me."

"I missed that headline," Liv related, taking another step back, now almost even with the wall.

"Of course you did. I put fences all around the country-side of Budapest."

"Why?" Liv asked, watching as the chicken finished outlining the circle on the stone floor and came to stand beside her. She still didn't know what the chicken had in mind or why Bellator had tugged her back to this spot, only releasing her when she was on the other side of the circle.

"Because it was funny," Cheverone said, still laughing.

"All the farmers came out, and there were lines of fences stretching every which way for miles."

"So you boxed them in?" Liv asked.

He shook his head. "No, I left gaps in the fences in places. It was too difficult to make it seamless."

"Again, why did you do that?" Liv asked, sort of entertained by this nut job.

"Because it made me legendary!"

"Ummm…I think it just made you a moron who wasted magical energy that could have been used for doing good."

The crazy glint in his eyes deepened. "There is no good in the world. There are only displays of power. The Dequiem collection has been my source of strength for a long time, and neither you nor Subner can take it from me. I'm too powerful." He lifted his hand, and with it, Liv rose off her feet.

"Damn it!" she growled, kicking. "Not one of these types of spells again. I hate being swept off my feet. It's so degrading."

"Now, because I'm a kind and thoughtful sorcerer," Cheverone began, "I plan to feed you to my other pet first. Then your chicken. That way, you don't have to watch it die."

"Other pet?" Liv asked, trying to free herself from the hold he had on her but unable to make much progress.

"Naturally," he said with a hiss as another anaconda's head skulked into the archway at his back.

"Oh, you have two snakes," Liv grumbled. "I guess two is just as much work as one. They keep themselves occupied, is that right?"

Cheverone cast his narrowed eyes on the snake. "She's stalling, but I can't really blame her."

Liv's eyes flicked to the chicken, which was pecking something else out in the dust on the floor.

"What do you mean, you're not hungry?" Cheverone asked the snake, which Liv hadn't heard say anything.

"I get that," Cheverone continued. "That was why I originally had De Soto go after them." He motioned to the beheaded snake lying in the distance. "As you can see, that didn't work out so well."

The anaconda hissed angrily, rising higher.

"Don't worry," Cheverone said matter-of-factly to the snake. "I'll get you another friend. Just kill them first."

The snake apparently didn't like Cheverone's insensitive manner. It turned on him, rising even higher into the air.

Just then, Liv recognized what the clever chicken was sketching on the floor. It was a picture of the room they were standing in. However, she'd added a few details, and as Liv glanced around, she realized exactly what the chicken wanted her to do.

The magician held up his hand, freezing the snake. "Don't forget who has the power here."

His act of immobilizing the snake released Liv, who tumbled to the floor. Landing with a thud, Liv hurled a ball of magical energy at the center of the circle the chicken had drawn, which she now realized indicated that a support column was missing. The place where it had been was only a discolored spot on the floor in the middle of the circle.

Cheverone and the snake swung to face Liv as the ball

of energy hit the floor under their feet, making it split in two. It opened like a massive cavern, and the structure around them shook. Liv plastered herself to the wall, worried that the floor under their feet would crumble into the water below them as it was doing to Cheverone and his snake.

It was the Cloaca Maxima; Rome's sewer system, which ran under the city and was more like a river than the pipelines Liv was used to.

Liv was unsure if it was going to work as Cheverone scrambled for the archway where he'd entered. The bricks were dissolving under his feet, but he was moving fast. And then the anaconda reached out with its long tail and wrapped it around Cheverone's body, squeezing him tight.

"What are you doing, you piece of shit?!" the magician roared, his face going red from the pressure. The snake had bound his arms to his side.

Liv actually wasn't sure what the snake was going to do. Rescue his master? Fling him across the room at her? Or lash across the hole in the middle of the room, which had thankfully stopped growing wider. The pressure point the chicken had indicated was perfect. It opened a perfectly symmetrical hole. The brownish waters of the Cloaca Maxima churned under their feet, sending up an unpleasant smell.

The snake's green eyes glowed in her direction. Liv prepared to use Bellator, although she was standing on a narrow ledge with little space to swing the sword. What she needed was to edge to the wider part of the floor, but the chicken was blocking her way, its eyes locked on the snake.

Liv was about to step over the bird when the anaconda's head plunged into the waters of the Cloaca Maxima, diving with a strange grace. It slipped soundlessly through the large opening, taking Cheverone with it.

"No!" the magician yelled, his face contorted with fear and disbelief as he disappeared into the dark waters.

"Eat shit and die, asshole," Liv said, letting out a sigh of relief.

CHAPTER THIRTEEN

"That was pretty smart planning you did," Liv remarked to the chicken as they stepped through the portal into Roya Lane.

The chicken didn't answer. Instead, she flapped her wings as she tried to avoid nearly getting trampled by the crowd.

"Oh, sorry," Liv stated, bending over and picking up the bird. "I forgot that you need to be carried some of the time."

Because they were in a congested area, Liv was surprised when Plato materialized beside her. She blinked at him, unsure she was actually seeing the lynx.

"What are you doing here?" she asked him.

"Telling you that you're being followed again," he said in a hushed voice.

Liv glanced around. "Adler is here?"

He nodded. "Yes, but he hasn't caught sight of you yet. He's been hiding in disguise over there, waiting to see you come through, and I guess hoping to follow you to Subner's shop."

"How did he know to look for me here?"

"I'm guessing he looked up your portal magic after the first time I gave him the slip for you."

Liv shook her head. "That man is up to something this time."

"I agree," Plato said, mostly in a whisper. There was so much going on that no one was paying them any attention. Besides, more curious than the fact that Liv was talking to a cat was, she was holding a chicken.

"I'm not sure I'll be able to sneak by him," Liv said, studying the lane. "I have to walk right by the area where he is, and it appears the crowd thins out there."

"Which is why he picked it, I'm sure," Plato stated. "But don't worry, I've got you covered. Just give me one minute, and then you can continue to Subner's."

"What are you going to do?" Liv asked curiously.

He lifted an eyebrow and gave her an incredulous glare.

"Okay, fine, you don't have to let the cat out of the bag," she said with a laugh.

Plato rolled his eyes. "I'm going to keep helping you even though those jokes are costing me lives."

"Because they are so funny?" Liv asked.

"Yes, that's it."

"Well, thanks for helping me give Adler the slip again," Liv said. "And for putting up with my bad jokes."

"Liv, if I was going to abandon you because of bad jokes, I would have been gone a long time ago."

She grimaced at him and lifted the chicken. "Rosella happens to like my jokes."

The bird squawked twice.

"Yes, she absolutely loves them," Plato agreed dryly.

"Hey, I bet you know what her name is, don't you?"

"Yes, and you're not even remotely close."

"Camila? Eva? Isabella?"

Plato shook his head.

"Well, don't tell me and spoil the fun," Liv said.

"You know I wasn't going to," Plato remarked.

"No, that would be too easy. Instead, I'm going to start calling her Chicken-Lady."

Plato's eyes studied the chicken before returning to Liv. "She doesn't like that."

"How do you know?" Liv asked. "She didn't make a peep."

Plato rolled his eyes again.

"Okay, sorry, that actually *was* a bad joke," Liv admitted.

"They are all bad jokes," Plato stated. "And I just know. Since you don't know her name—"

"And you and Papa Creola won't tell me," Liv cut in.

"And you can't figure it out on your own," Plato went on, "she'd prefer for you to call her 'the Scientist.'"

"What?" Liv exclaimed. "Even in the magical world, I'll look like a loon if I refer to a chicken as a scientist."

Plato shook his head at the chicken. "No, I don't know how to make her stop. It's like this weird savant thing she does."

"Yes, my special power is making puns," Liv said, scowling at the animals. "And how do *you* know what she wants to be called?"

When Plato didn't answer, Liv threw up her free hand. "Fine, fine. Don't tell me. I'll just carry around the chicken and call her 'Scientist.' Maybe I can carry you around in my other arm and call you 'Teacher' or 'Guru.' I think then I'll get some attention."

"You know I don't like to be carried," Plato said simply.

"And you have to go and run interference for me." Liv pointed to where Adler was.

"Yes, and it might take me a little longer than I thought if it works at all. The crowd dynamic has shifted since we've been talking."

"Hey, I need you to stay paws-itive," Liv said, slapping her knee as she chuckled.

Plato blinked impassively at her.

"Okay, when will I know it's safe to continue down Roya Lane?" Liv asked.

"You'll know," he said simply and disappeared into the crowd.

Liv shook her head at the chicken. "Isn't he cute?"

The bird didn't apparently have a response to this. At least not one that Liv could understand since she didn't have telepathy or whatever it was that let Plato know things.

She was considering her options for gaining such a skill when a ruckus down the lane stole her attention. A woman's voice echoed down the path as the crowd swept forward.

"Get away from me!" the woman yelled as a loud growl sounded from somewhere near her.

"Help her!" someone yelled.

"Here, we'll surround them," someone else called as the crowd turned into a wall around where Adler had been stationed, apparently disguised as a woman.

Liv ducked and sprinted past, heading for Subner's shop before the distraction was over.

CHAPTER FOURTEEN

The entire way down Roya Lane, Liv kept checking over her shoulder. Thankfully she didn't notice Adler or an old lady, only a ton of commotion at the far end. Who knew what Plato had done to buy her the time, and he obviously wasn't going to tell her.

The Fantastical Armory's doors were open when Liv entered, carrying the chicken and the bag of swords.

Subner glanced up from his book, a pair of reading spectacles on his face. "There you are. It took you long enough."

"That's a strange way of saying 'thank you,'" Liv said, unshouldering the bag full of swords.

"You left here a day ago," he grumbled.

"To go and find weapons when you had zero ideas where they might be or who took them?" Liv argued.

"How do you know you were successful?"

"Does the name Cheverone ring any bells?"

Subner scowled. "He didn't! That old so-and-so. I bet he didn't even use any of the swords."

"No, he said he wanted the Dequiem set for their power reserves."

Subner nodded like this made perfect sense. "Such a coward. He stole an arsenal even though he doesn't know how to swing a sword. I hope you made him pay."

Liv gave the chicken a sideways look. "Let's just say he's feeling pretty shitty right about now."

Subner opened the small bag, peering inside. His mouth fell open, and he hustled for the back countertop. "It's really them! The Dequiem set."

"You're welcome," Liv said, an uncertain tone in her voice.

One by one, Subner pulled the swords from the bag, admiring each individually. "They all appear to be here, too."

"I agree that I did an amazing job recovering your mysterious objects," Liv teased.

Subner ignored her, continuing to gawk over his collection.

"If you're looking for a thank you from him, you'll be waiting a long time," Papa Creola said by her side, having magically appeared.

"Does that mean several minutes or years or what?" Liv asked. "I realize time is relative for you."

He didn't seem to enjoy her joke. "Gnomes don't waste time showing gratitude."

"No wonder they are so grumpy," Liv stated, then covered half her face. "Not you, though, Papa Creola. You're a beam of sunshine."

It was true. Papa Creola was almost chipper-looking in

comparison to other gnomes with his round, rosy cheeks and twinkling eyes.

He dismissed her with a wave of his hand. "I do appreciate that you recovered Subner's weapons for him. The place is a bit bare, and this will help with bringing in business."

Liv glanced around at the empty shop, looking for a place to set Scientist down. "So, I have your chicken alive. What's next?"

Papa Creola seemed to have a silent conversation with the bird before glancing at Liv, nodding his head. It was starting to frustrate her that everyone but her could do that. "The person inside this chicken is the only one who knows where an evil magician is. He's the one who forced her to create the illegal magical-tech devices. His name is Shitkphace."

A laugh burst from Liv's mouth. "You want me to go after a villain named Shitface?"

Papa Creola didn't appear amused. "His name is Shitkphace. The 'k' is silent."

"Okay, but I'm going to have a hard time keeping a straight face while taking down Shitface."

"I'm guessing that you never keep a straight face, ever," Papa Creola stated. "Anyway, I don't know where Shitkphace is hiding." He pointed at the chicken. "Only she does."

"Well, can't you communicate with her?" Liv asked.

He gave her an appalled look. "Of course, I can't. She's currently a chicken."

"Oh, well, I just assumed you two were having silent

telepathic conversations like she has with Plato," Liv related.

"Plato is a different kind of being, and he doesn't play by the same rules that govern most of us.

Liv let out a long breath, a bit overwhelmed that Plato was violating rules even Father Time had to follow.

"Anyway, this scientist is the only one who knows where Shitkphace is located. I've been busy rounding up the magical-tech devices he had her make, but he's figured out how to replicate the design. As long as he's out there, he'll keep creating tech that messes with the fabric of time."

"Okay, so can you change Scientist?" Liv asked.

"No, I can't," Papa Creola answered. "The only person I believe can safely do it is a fae by the name of Phillippe Foggerbottom—"

"Who are these people's parents? Why are they so bad at naming their children?" Liv asked.

Papa Creola ignored her comment. "Phillippe isn't going to want to help you."

"Shocking," Liv said with zero emotions.

"He's the only one I trust to turn the scientist back, though," Papa Creola continued. "You see, he was once a master of transfiguration."

"Once?" Liv asked, enjoying too much how this was all unfolding.

"He has since taken a different position in the mortal world," Papa Creola continued.

"Okay, so I have to threaten him until he turns Scientist back, right?"

Papa Creola shook his head.

"You're going to send me with a note that says you'll

dock his life by a few hundred years if he doesn't do what I say?" Liv guessed.

"No, I'm afraid that death is what the old fae is looking forward to most."

"Wow, he sounds like a real cheerful person," Liv jested.

"He isn't, and that will probably be one of your biggest obstacles to getting his cooperation."

"Well, how am I going to get him to turn the chicken back?" Liv asked.

"He won't listen to me, but all fae are loyal to their king, no matter what," Papa Creola stated.

Liv dropped her chin and regarded him with a hooded expression. "You're not implying…"

The old gnome nodded. "I am. King Rudolfus is the only one who can force Phillippe Foggerbottom to do what we want. Do you think you can get him to make that decree?"

Liv sighed. "Yes, but it will cost me several hundred brain cells and probably make me want to take a sledge-hammer to my head."

Papa Creola cracked the tiniest of smiles. "That's the effect Rudolfus Sweetwater has on me as well, so better you than me."

Liv went to retrieve the chicken. "Yeah, thanks, Pops."

CHAPTER FIFTEEN

"Oh, are *you* in for a treat," Liv said, stepping through the portal into the kingdom of the fae, also known as the Las Vegas Strip.

The chicken didn't look impressed, only slightly agitated by the cigarette smoke that wafted over them as obnoxious tourists jostled by, their heads craned up to look at the buildings towering overhead. Many had their phones out and were snapping pictures of the lights or selfies as they posed in front of the Bellagio's fountain.

"You know what? Maybe I shouldn't presume you haven't met Rudolf Sweetwater," Liv said to the chicken. "He does get around. Far less these days, but still, I believe he spent a few centuries whoring around."

Scientist squawked with offense.

"I'm not insinuating that you're easy," Liv amended. "I'm simply saying it's possible that he would have made a pass at you or offended your intelligence somehow. That's what he's best at."

As soon as they entered the Cosmopolitan Hotel, Liv recognized the many fae who pretended to work as mortals, their wings glamoured.

"Hey, I need to see the king," she said to a waiter who was cleaning a cocktail table.

The fae looked her over in her black cape and stringy hair and shook his head. "Is he expecting you, magician?"

"No, but that shouldn't matter," she stated. "He likes it when I surprise him."

The man gave a humorless laugh. "We understand that you want to meet the newest king of the fae, but we can't have every magician who strolls in off the street pestering him." His eyes slid to the chicken. "Especially ones who have strange pets."

"This isn't my pet," Liv argued. "I have a talking cat. And Rudolf will want to see me. I'm on his advisory board. I was at his coronation. Don't you recognize me?"

The fae eyed her again. "No, I don't."

Liv growled. She had looked quite different at the coronation. If only she had her summoning stone, then this wouldn't be a problem. She could call Rudolf straight to her side without having to deal with this dimwit.

"Look, I'm a Warrior for the House of Seven, and I suggest you take me to Rudolf. Otherwise, when I do see him, I'm going to tell him to clip your wings and cut your ration of Nutella."

The man covered the gasp about to escape his mouth. "Very well. We will take you up there, but if you're not allowed to see the king, then you've sealed your miserable fate."

Three fae dressed in suits strode over at once.

"Just you wait, you oversized fairy," Liv threatened. Next time she'd need a more direct way of finding Rudolf. She just hadn't had a chance to touch base with him since he'd taken over the empire. She wasn't even sure if his throne room was in the same place as Queen Visa's had been, but regardless, she knew it would be heavily guarded.

"I thought I was being respectful by asking to see the king," Liv whispered to the chicken as the waiter lead the way through the casino, the guards striding behind her, "but now I realize they just thought I was a quack."

The chicken lowered her head and covered it with her wing.

"You're doing that because of the noise and smoke and not because of my awesome joke, right?"

Scientist didn't answer.

Once out of the elevator, Liv realized they were going to the same place where Queen Visa's chambers had been located. However, things looked quite different. Instead of the posh, monochromatic decor of his predecessor, Rudolf had used a more modern, Gen X approach.

The plaster and moldings on the walls had been covered with unstained wood. Overhead, the rafters were exposed, and the fixtures were brushed steel.

"Whoa, I left my hipster card at home," Liv said to the chicken, loud enough for the security guards to hear.

The fae in front of her swung around, a pursed expression on his face. "His Excellency is making us more relevant by taking us out of the dark ages and innovating our spirit through ingenuity."

"I will give you a hundred dollars if you can tell me in laymen's terms what that means," Liv challenged.

The man's mouth fell open. Shut again. He looked behind her at the guards as if searching for answers. "I-I-It is complicated to explain."

Liv shrugged, striding around the fae. "I get that babbling big words is fun, but without meaning, they are useless."

The guards caught up with her right away, two of them throwing their arms in front of her, blocking the way.

Liv smirked, enjoying this game. "I know my way from here, boys. No need for the escort."

"Your presence hasn't been approved by the king," the first fae said with a disapproving look on his face.

Liv waved at the tall set of double doors in front of them. "Okay, then. Let's ask your king if it's okay that I came to play."

The fae took off once more, struggling to open the heavy doors. When he was able to get one back, Liv was both impressed and slightly repulsed by the industrial appearance of the throne room. The floor was all stained concrete. Overhead, the ductwork was all exposed. Light-bulbs hung from the ceiling, and the walls were all exposed brick.

On one side of the large room was a minimalist bar. Behind it was a man serving drinks, who had a handlebar mustache and was wearing a black vest over his wrinkled button-up shirt.

The fae strewn around the room were attired very differently than the last time Liv was there. They didn't sport skimpy dresses or flamboyant suits. Instead, almost all of them were wearing skinny jeans rolled up at the ankles. The men wore suspenders, and many of the girls had cropped haircuts and baby bangs. The fae were sitting upright on tufted couches or in uncomfortable metal chairs, having subdued conversations.

"Where have you brought me?" Liv asked, panic in her voice. "Am I in North Hollywood? Please tell me we didn't portal to that hipster sanctuary, because I can't control my anger when those types go on and on about non-profit organizations and bringing back the accordion."

Ignoring her, the fae in front of her led them through the room. At the back, instead of the throne that had been there before, there was a poor excuse for a desk. It was mostly unpolished wood and large metal bolts. Sitting behind it was Rudolf, his back toward them as he leaned back in a swivel chair.

"Tell them I want a better supplier of organic vegan peanuts," he said into the phone, not sounding at all like himself.

After a pause, he responded, "That's what they want you to believe. However, I've had peanuts that I'm certain had questionable origins."

He clicked off the phone.

The fae who had led them in cleared his throat to get the king's attention. Rudolf spun around, a smile lighting his eyes. He covered it quickly, turning his head to the side with a sly expression.

"Your Majesty, this magician has told us that she knows you and you would want to see her," the fae explained. "Please tell us whether we should allow her to stay or escort her from the property."

Rudolf's mouth fell open as he sat up. He had grown a long beard, and his hair on the side of his head was shaved, just like a disgusting hipster. And even stranger was that he was wearing thick-rimmed glasses. "You! How dare you show your face here, Biv Leaufont!"

CHAPTER SIXTEEN

Liv lowered her chin, realizing immediately the game of power Rudolf was playing. "Ummm, seriously? You're not doing this, are you, Ru?"

He winked, standing to reveal that he was wearing a short-sleeved shirt buttoned all the way to his neck, a bowtie, high-waisted jeans, and suspenders. "I am. And you know why!"

"Because you're bored and want me to kick these guard's asses?" Liv guessed.

He smirked. "That's exactly right." Turning his attention to the first fae, he clapped his hands on his cheeks. "Oh, no. You've allowed a dangerous assassin in here. Get her before it's too late."

All three of the guards at Liv's back reached for her. Sensing this, she dropped to the ground, rolling to the side. Once on her feet, she set the chicken down and immediately threw a punch into the first guard's stomach. Another one threw up his palm a second later and ball of ice surged toward her.

Liv held up her own hand, sending a fireball to meet the ice. They met in the air, each dissolving at once. While the fae was off guard, Liv sent a rush of wind at him, knocking him onto one of the empty sofas, where his legs flew over his head, making him topple over the side.

The last guard had thought he'd snuck up behind her, but she grabbed him around the neck, spinning him until he was in a headlock.

"Is this what you wanted?" Liv asked, looking straight at Rudolf.

He tapped his foot, arms in front of his chest as he nodded. "Yes, that was exactly what I've been needing to liven up things in here."

"Call off your men, or in the next round, there will be blood," Liv warned.

He nodded. "Very well." Directing his gaze to the closest guard, whom Liv had punched, Rudolf shook his head. "Never mind. I thought this was one of my nemeses, but it turns out it's actually my best friend, Liv Beaufont. Silly me. I always get them confused."

As if used to these antics, the nearest guard pressed his lips together and nodded. The guard who had toppled over the couch stood, brushing himself off. Liv released the one in the headlock, pushing him away just in case he didn't know how to take orders. He backed away from her immediately.

"You can go, boys," Rudolf said, waving the four fae away. "And please don't hassle Liv the next time she wants to visit me."

"Which will be never," Liv remarked, picking up the chicken.

"Oh, come on," Rudolf stated. "You're on my council. I'll need your help."

"You need your head checked."

"Can I really be blamed for wanting to see your moves?" Rudolf asked. "I knew you'd handle them fast and keep them humble."

"What if they were better fighters than me?" Liv asked.

"That's impossible." He pointed at the chicken. "Did you bring me a housewarming present? I've been thinking of adding a chicken coop on the roof. There's nothing better than fresh eggs."

"No." Liv set the chicken on Rudolf's desk. "But the chicken is why I'm here."

"Well, before we get to all that, we should catch up properly." He hooked his arm through hers, taking her over to what she now realized was a DJ booth. The hipster behind the desk had three Apple computers and a record player in front of him. "Willard, play me some vinyl, would you?"

The fae gave Rudolf a thumbs-up. "Of course. I've got a new jam from a band that no one has ever heard of. Their chords are really smooth, but I think they are about to get signed by a major recording studio."

Rudolf nodded. "You're allowed to play them until they get big. Then we smash all their records and scoff when people mention them."

"Yes, my king," the man answered, laying a record on the player.

Still leading Liv, Rudolf directed her to the bar. "Would you like a PBR, or maybe something a little more feminine, like an organic orange crush with cloves and a hint of bathtub whiskey?"

"What I'd like is to punch you in the beard," Liv said, tugging her arm loose.

Rudolf stroked his hand through his beard, grinning. "You like it, don't you?"

"No," Liv answered at once. "And why are you wearing glasses? I thought fae had perfect vision."

"We do," Rudolf agreed. "I thought they looked good. They are ironic glasses because I don't really need them. Don't you think they make me look smart?"

"I'm not sure there is anything on this planet that can make you look smart. Well, unless you're standing next to Serena. She kind of makes you look sort of smart."

"Just like a good woman should," Rudolf related.

"Now I want to know what the hell is going on here? You said you were going to make good changes for the fae, not turn the kingdom into Portland, Oregon. Please, please tell me you haven't added kale to every menu on the Strip and required that all the computers be replaced with type-writers?"

Rudolf's gaze dropped to the ground. "It's really uncanny how you know things about me. It's like we're the same person."

"No, we're not, because I have a brain in my head, and you're a freaking idiot."

The bartender slid two cans of Pabst Blue Ribbon across the counter to Rudolf. He caught them, handing one to Liv. "I thought I'd try something different. Queen Visa was so materialistic. I'm trying a different approach. One that's more—"

"Ridiculous?" Liv asked, cutting him off.

"One that's less about conformity," he corrected.

She shook her head. "No, you're just exchanging one type of materialism for another. Before, your people could only wear the top designers and rock out to EDM. Now they have to wear American Apparel and Ray-Ban sunglasses and only watch indie movies. Have you tried just letting them be themselves?"

"Do you really think that could work?" Rudolf asked, opening his can of beer.

Liv nodded, doing the same. "Of course, it could. You'd be surprised who people are when you allow them to do what they want." A second later, she added, "Within reason."

Rudolf took a sip. "I just thought my people were looking at me to give them something."

"They are," she reasoned. "They want leadership, resources, and support. What they *don't* need is you telling them they must garden their own vegetables and only eat vegan food." She took a drink of the beer and spat it out. "Why is this warm?"

"It supposed to taste better like that," Rudolf answered.

Liv shoved the can of beer at him. "Seriously, do what feels good, not what some dumb culture of pretentious hipsters says is right." She glanced around at the decorations. "Do you actually like the way this place looks?"

Rudolf gave her a guilty expression. "Not really. And my desk is super uncomfortable. And this beard itches horribly."

"Then will you please get rid of it all and decorate this

place the way you like it, rather than how some supposed 'cool kids' think it should look?"

"Okay, you're right," Rudolf said as Serena trotted over, casting a questioning look at the chicken.

"I think one of those pigeons from the roof got in," the mortal said.

"That's a chicken," Liv corrected.

Serena gave her a fake smile. "It's so good to see you again, Liv. I'm happy you're here because Rudolf told me that I should be since you helped us mend things when we had a fight before the coronation."

"Wow," Liv said with zero inflection. "That didn't seem at all rehearsed."

Serena flipped her long brown hair off her shoulder. "And I don't hate you for constantly coming around and flaunting your supposed magical powers and prestige as a soldier for the Hut of Seven."

"You do realize that you're using your out-loud voice again, right?" Liv asked the mortal.

She merely blinked back at her.

"And my magical powers aren't supposed," Liv began. "And I'm a Warrior for the House of Seven, but that's a lot for you to remember, so we'll take it in chunks. Can you say 'warrior?'"

As if she couldn't, Serena shook her head, giving her attention to Rudolf. "The water company called and said that replacing the taps with champagne probably won't work."

"Hold up," Liv said, stepping forward. "You're trying to do what?"

Serena shot her a hostile expression. "Rudolf said I can implement a few of my ideas."

"Because I encouraged him not to shut you down," Liv argued, trying to get the dimwit to see her logic.

"So you say," Serena responded. "Anyway, I have three projects I'm trying to push through. One is for an energy source that can be found underground. I'm thinking we can use it to fuel our vehicles."

"It's called oil, and it's already been done," Liv stated dryly.

"Then I'd like to replace the water in our pipes with champagne," Serena went on.

"Which has so many issues, I can't even figure out where to start," Liv said.

"And if I have time, I'd like to implement brand-new cold fusion technology into all the casinos. It could save the electrical power plants over ninety percent every single year," Serena said, mostly sounding bored.

"Yes!" Liv cheered. "Now you have an idea. Go with that one! Do it."

Suddenly looking excited by Liv's reaction, Serena smiled. "If you like that idea, I also had one where we'd replace the lights in the hotel bathrooms with tanning lamps. That way, our guests can get a tan while they are getting ready. Pretty ingenious, huh?"

Liv let out a defeated breath. "I really wished you would have stopped while you were ahead, but I get that not all ideas can be gold."

"Serena has many, many more," Rudolf said proudly, wrapping his arm around her shoulder.

"All of which should be checked by me first," Liv stated.

"As one of your trusted advisors, I think you should give me the responsibility of reviewing all of these before they are implemented."

"You're not going to steal them, are you?" Serena asked with a glare.

"I wouldn't dream of it," Liv stated, pointing at the chicken. "Have you had a chance to meet Scientist? I bet she'd like to hear about your ideas."

Serena did a double-take at the chicken. "Is that what scientists look like? I've never met one before." She leaned forward, cupping her mouth to whisper to the side. "To be honest, I thought that was a type of bird."

Liv gave her a mock expression of shock. "No!"

Serena nodded. "I did. But I'll totally go and share my ideas with the scientist."

"If she squawks, it means to keep talking," Liv yelled to Serena as the mortal strode in the chicken's direction.

"She really is something special," Rudolf said, smiling at the mortal as she retreated.

"She's very special," Liv agreed.

"So speaking of ideas," Rudolf began, "I've started a few corporations. I'd like to get out of the gambling business and invest our resources into making the fae's fortunes, centered around a foodie conglomeration."

"Say what?" Liv asked.

"Well, gambling and overindulgence were the central pillars of the fae's culture."

"Which is how the Las Vegas Strip came to be," Liv added.

"Exactly," Rudolf agreed. "However, like we've talked about, I want my people to use their talents. I was thinking we could create a line of keto-friendly power bars and then branch out from there. Low-carb chips, no-calorie wine, and maybe cake that impregnates."

"Again, I'm going to need this list of ideas," Liv stated. "However, I like them, for the most part. I think healthful eating should be encouraged. And mortals will eat up keto-friendly products."

Rudolf gave her a disappointed look. "I don't approve of the pun."

"Seriously, you of all people are against my jokes now?" Liv asked. "I really can't win with anyone."

Liv thought her eyes were deceiving her when a giant she recognized strode through the door behind Rudolf's desk. "Rory? What are you doing here?"

CHAPTER SEVENTEEN

Thankfully the giant wasn't wearing a dumb beard or a tank top. He appeared like his normal self. However, Liv was instantly worried that he had a fever and was lost and disoriented.

His eyes glanced up from a folder in his hands. He appeared a bit lost. "Liv, what are you doing here?"

"I'm trying to get Rudolf's help with the chicken, who apparently wants to be called Scientist," Liv stated, pointing at the bird.

Rory glanced over to where Serena was incessantly babbling to the bird. "Oh, so you still don't know her name."

"I know she's a magician from Italy, so I'm making progress," Liv explained. "Now, what are you doing here? Did Rudolf drug and abduct you? He only did that to me once."

Rudolf covered his face. "I can't believe you broke my nose. I simply wanted to surprise you."

"I don't like waking up on the floor of a speakeasy hours before they're supposed to open," Liv explained.

Rudolf huffed. "I know that now. But that's how you ensure you get the best places in a busy joint."

Liv shook this off and focused on Rory. "Seriously, what are you doing here?"

"I'm helping Rudolf with his new corporation," Rory answered.

Liv's brow scrunched up. "How? Why? I actually have so many questions right now that my head is about to explode."

"Well, Ronald's specialty is something we're in desperate need of," Rudolf stated.

"His name is Rory," Liv corrected. "And specialty?"

Rory elbowed the fae. "She doesn't know what I do for a living because she doesn't pay attention."

"Oh, my God!" Liv complained. "I've been battling madmen in ancient Roman ruins and slaughtering demons so you all can lollygag, but I get in trouble for not paying attention to some details about your profession that I believe you've yet to give."

Rudolf rolled his eyes, giving the giant a commiserating expression. "She doesn't know anything about me either. I had to tell her I was the king of this empire."

"I was there when you defeated Queen Visa and were automatically appointed," Liv stated, frustration evident in her tone.

"She's always got excuses," Rudolf stated, taking the report out of Rory's hand. "Oh, I see what you've done here. I like it."

Rory turned the report around. "It's upside-down."

Rudolf frowned. "Well, now it makes zero sense."

"Seriously, Ronald, what are you helping with? Just tell me what your profession is," Liv said.

"I'm helping the fae with their newest business ventures," Rory stated simply.

"By doing?" Liv encouraged.

"Rocket science, or so it seems," Rudolf told her, shutting the report folder. "Good work, my giant friend. You may take one or two of my fae as one of your servants."

"Rudolf…" Liv said in a punishing tone.

"Okay, you can't have them. But I'll pay you for your services if that's at all acceptable," Rudolf amended.

"Yes, that's fine," Rory stated. "I'll set it up so it goes to my offshore account and isn't traceable, like all the other transmissions from the fae."

"Why do I feel like I'm in a weird, wacky funhouse?" Liv asked.

"You didn't drink the tap water, did you?" Rudolf asked, sudden concern in his voice. "We might have experimented with some things before Serena had the awesome idea for champagne water."

"That wasn't a good idea," Liv corrected.

"Right," Rudolf stated. "I remember that now. Anyway, before she'd had me magick a hair straightener into the water supply so that everyone could have smooth locks. Then we remembered that people drink the water and not just shower in it. We're working on fixing it."

"Yeah, that's a hard thing to remember," Liv stated.

"So you had a request for me, my bestie?" Rudolf asked.

Liv scratched her head, having strangely forgotten her reason for subjecting herself to all this irritation. She caught sight of the chicken. "Oh, yeah. That's right. I need you to make a decree that one of your fae, a Mr. Phillippe Foggerbottom, does what I ask."

Rudolf's face lit up. "Oh, a little dating experiment. I knew you'd want to play the field sooner or later. But you're okay-looking, so I'm sure you don't have to make me force a fae to go out with you. Well, okay, maybe a fae, but not a magician. They are pretty desperate."

Liv lowered her chin, thinking she should have expected this. "I need the fae to turn the scientist chicken back into its normal form."

"And then go out with you?" Rudolf asked.

"Nope," Liv answered. "I'm not looking for a date at all."

"So this visit was purely business?" Rudolf sounded disappointed.

"Yes, why?" Liv asked.

"Well, I was just hoping… It's fine," Rudolf stated. "But I can't help you unless you agree to do something for me."

"Wait," Liv complained. "You said you were done with these agreements. I didn't think I'd be indebted to you for favors anymore."

"Well, you were wrong," Rudolf corrected.

Liv felt the heat boiling to the surface. "Rudolf Sweetwater, I've had just about as much of your bullshit as I can take!"

All the fae in the room turned to watch the spectacle. Liv was just about to stomp on Rudolf's blindingly white Converse shoes when he held up his hand. "I was simply going to request that you be my best man at my wedding. I'm sorry if that's me asking too much. I'll do whatever you need with no requests."

Liv halted. Tilted her head to the side. "You get that I'm not a man, right?"

He waved her off. "You haven't gotten there yet. I see a future, though, where you embrace—"

"Don't finish that sentence or I'll turn you inside-out using a potato peeler," Liv stated.

He nodded. "And yes, I'd like you to be my best man at my wedding. Please say you'll do it."

Liv considered that. It would probably be something she regretted, but as she looked into Rudolf's blue eyes, she couldn't say no. "Yeah, fine. I'll do it."

He snapped his fingers, a rolled-up piece of parchment materializing. "And as always, I'll always fulfill your request. Unless it requires me taking it up the—"

"I request that you not finish that sentence." Liv plucked the decree from his fingers.

CHAPTER EIGHTEEN

Liv waited for Papa Creola to send Phillippe Foggerbottom's information to her codex. For being the Father of Time, he wasn't really punctual about things.

"So, are you excited to get your body back?" Liv asked the chicken as they sat in a rooftop bar overlooking the Strip. She couldn't stand one more minute in that industrial hipster palace. Rory had buzzed off, mumbling something about drafting some reports, and Rudolf had said it was time for his morning headstand. He wouldn't listen to reason when Liv told him it was midafternoon. That was when she'd decided she could use some fresh air and a shot of whiskey while she waited for Father "Takes His Time."

The chicken, who didn't appear comfortable occupying a barstool at the busy venue, simply glanced around. Liv wasn't at all put off by the man-children with too much testosterone jockeying for the attention of one of the many girls wearing too much makeup and hair extensions. Maybe the whiskey was making it easier for Liv to tolerate the mouth-breathers who usually put her on edge when they were too close.

Liv felt the rush of something breeze by her head. A second later, a blade with an ivory handle stuck in the wall behind the bar.

"There you are, Warrior!" someone yelled. "Prepare to die."

The crowd around Liv dispersed at once. Still, she hardly did more than blink. Giving the chicken a casual expression, she picked up her whiskey. "Would you mind hopping behind this bar while I take care of some trash?"

The chicken didn't answer, only jumped up on the bar and disappeared over the other side.

If only everyone would be so cooperative, Liv thought as she took a sip of her drink. Damn, it was good whiskey, and she sort of wanted to finish it, but it wasn't the kind you slammed. Hopefully, this jerk who was standing at her back wouldn't take long to kill. She wiped the side of her mouth, conscious that mortals were staring at her from a distance, probably wondering why she wasn't reacting immediately to the threat at her back. The reason was simple. Whoever was behind her didn't want to put a knife in her back. That was evident by the expert skills he'd used to throw the knife. No, whoever this was wanted to look at her in the eyes when he killed her. Too bad for him that he was going to die first.

Liv set down her half-drunk whiskey, her other hand sliding instinctively to Bellator. Pushing back the barstool, Liv pulled the sword from its sheath in one fluid movement.

The figure standing squarely in front of her, only

fifteen feet away, wasn't someone she'd encountered before. He was an elf with long whitish-green hair who looked about Liv's age, although he was probably several hundred years old. Damn elves and their anti-aging properties.

The elf wore beautiful leather armor, a clunky belt, and riding boots. One of his hands was resting on the hilt of the sword

as he stood casually, one foot in front of the other.

He was actually sort of cute, with his mirrored green eyes and high cheekbones. *Well, he would be cute, but there was that whole trying to kill me thing*, Liv thought.

His hand flexed by his side as his lips spread in a long line, he said, "You've been looking for me, haven't you?"

Liv's eyes darted up and to the right as she thought. "No, I don't think so."

"Well, here I finally am." With practiced grace, the elf swung the sword up, tossing it to his other hand. It came across, meeting Bellator in midair.

"Who exactly are you?" Liv asked between measured breaths, blocking the next two attacks.

The elf cackled, looking around at the crowd like they might join in with him. "As if you don't know."

Liv shoved the elf back but he made up the space quickly. "No, seriously I don't know."

As if fighting her was barely keeping him awake, the elf sauntered to the right, bringing his sword dangerously close to Liv's face. "You've spent all this effort to track me down, and now you pretend as if you don't know who I am."

Instead of slicing her face off, the elf merely grabbed

her by the back of her jacket and launched her into a pair of chairs next to the pool. "Are you the one who made Inexorabilis?"

"What?" the elf asked in response, slicing his blade through the air. Liv rolled to the side just before it struck the table next to her.

The elf struggled to pull the sword back out since it had gone all the way through the table, catching in the metal legs. She used this moment to kick the elves' legs out from underneath him. He landed on his backside but quickly recovered, springing straight to his feet.

"Seriously, mister," Liv stated, stepping sideways as the elf copied her movement. "I don't know who you are."

"Oh, Warrior, I know it is you who has been asking around about me," the elf said.

Liv was about to attack while he was weaponless, but in a flash he ran forward, grabbing the hilt of his protruding sword. In a beautiful display of power, he ran up the side of a chair, still holding onto the sword and back-flipped around, yanking the blade free. The elf landed on the edge of the table, making it tilt forward, while he ran down it like a ramp, whipping his sword back and forth, craziness radiating from his mirrored eyes.

Liv brought Bellator around, but the maniac knocked it out of her hands at once, and it clattered across the floor and landed in the pool. The elf sent her down to the ground with a sudden jolt of magic. She was about to respond with a fireball when she realized that she was paralyzed from the head down. All she could do was blink.

The evil elf swiveled his sword around, pointing it at Liv's throat. She wanted to gulp or say something to either insult him or throw him off his game. Maybe both. Words were her greatest weapons.

"Any last words, Warrior?" the elf asked, vicious heat in his words.

Liv caught her reflection in his eyes. She had a reply ready, something fiery and insulting that would definitely turn the tables. As she opened her mouth to speak, an arrow went straight through the elf's head. He wavered for a moment as if he was momentarily surprised by this change in events, then he swayed to the left before falling to the right and landing on his side, his sword clattering to the ground with him.

CHAPTER NINETEEN

As soon as she was released, Liv bolted to her feet, creating a fireball at once and readying to launch it at whoever had the bow and arrow.

She froze.

Standing on the other side of the pool, his black cloak billowing in the wind, was none other than Stefan Ludwig. His black hair was matted over his forehead, his chin tucked, and a mischievous glint in his eyes.

He lowered the bow and regarded Liv with a sideways grin before turning to address the crowd. "That's all for now. Catch the full show later. Same spot, different actors. Until then, the rooftop is closed."

The mortals who had backed off a safe distance to watch the fight erupted into applause as Liv retrieved Bellator from the bottom of the pool using a summoning spell.

Chatting excitedly, the mortals dispersed.

Liv caught Stefan's eye as she strode back to the bar,

stepping over the dead elf's body. That was Stefan's problem.

Sheathing Bellator first, Liv hopped over the bar, popping up just as Stefan arrived on the other side, a proud grin on his face.

"You're welcome," he sang, winking at her.

"You were the Warrior asking about Mirror Eyes, weren't you?"

He slung his bow over his back and nodded. "Spincoster is the despicable elf's name." Stefan gestured casually over his shoulder at the dead body. "And yes, I was the one asking around about him, although I didn't think he'd go after you or another Warrior. Good thing I was tracking him. So again, you're welcome." He bowed slightly.

"I totally had the situation handled," Liv said, taking a sip of her whiskey, grateful that it hadn't been tossed.

"He had his sword to your throat," Stefan countered.

"I was about to talk my way back to a standing position," Liv argued.

"Although I believe you, I'm not sure trying to fight Spincoster would have worked," Stefan explained. "He's deadly with a sword. I would have never gone up against him like that, which was why I picked up this bow and arrow." He patted his quiver.

Liv regarded him over the glass in her hands. "I didn't really have a choice about going up against his sword, and he *was* pretty impressive. I would have definitely gotten nicked if we'd kept fighting."

"But I came to your rescue." Stefan pressed his hand to his chest proudly.

"You're looking for a thank you, aren't you?" Liv asked.

"I'm just happy to finally return the favor after all the times you've saved me."

"Should I remind you that I wouldn't have been in danger from Spincoster if not for you and your nosing around?"

He shrugged, putting his elbows on the bar and leaning forward. "I don't see any reason to bring that part up."

Liv shook her head and finished her drink.

"So since you're back there, you mind fixing me a drink?" Stefan asked.

Liv pulled out her codex, confirming that Papa Creola still hadn't sent the location for Foggerbottom. "Sure, why not? But first, I need you to hold something."

"Well, of course," Stefan answered, extending his hands over the bar.

Liv leaned down and picked up Scientist.

Stefan's face was sort of priceless when she put the chicken in his arms.

"Here, hold my chicken so I don't step on her," Liv said, going to work making drinks.

Stefan laughed. "You always say the most unpredictable things." He set the chicken down on the bar, where she promptly took a seat, looking up at him with what could only be described as instant adoration.

"You want a virgin strawberry daiquiri, right?" Liv asked, dropping ice cubes into two tumblers.

"With two limes, please," Stefan said, not missing a beat.

Liv poured two healthy doses of whiskey. "What are you going to do with your dead guy?" She nodded in the direction of Spincoster.

"Send his body back to the Kingdom of the Elves," he

said, giving her an appreciative look when she slid a glass in his direction.

"So this has something to do with your case? You weren't just trying to get me killed?" Liv asked, noticing that the chicken still hadn't taken her eyes off of Stefan.

"Getting you killed was never on the agenda," Stefan explained, taking a sip. "Spincoster was smarter than I gave him credit for. He got wind that I was asking about him and went after the closest Warrior he could find. That happened to be you, but what he didn't realize was that I was close behind him. That was when I stepped in earlier and saved your life. You remember that part?"

Liv sipped her drink. "Hardly."

"I'll make you a scrapbook to commemorate the occasion," Stefan fired back.

"Make sure it's on rose-scented paper or I'll throw it away," Liv warned.

"Of course. What do you take me for, some barbarian?" he asked with mock offense.

"You just fired an arrow across a chic pool on the rooftop of the Cosmopolitan, killing a really pretty elf," Liv stated blandly.

"Who, by the way, was a horrible villain, and one of the biggest dangers to the High Elf Council," Stefan explained.

"And that's why you went after him, wasn't it? To earn the favor of the High Elf Council so they'd sign the negotiation with the House of Seven?" Liv asked.

He tapped his fingers on the bar rhythmically. "Well, I asked myself, what would Liv Beaufont do?"

"If she was you, she'd clean under her damn nails," Liv said, nodding at his hands.

He glanced at his nails and shrugged. "Yes, I should wash up soon. I've been on the road for days. Maybe I'll get a room downstairs. I hear they are nice."

"Just don't drink the tap water," Liv warned.

"Why drink water when there's whiskey?" Stefan said, indicating his empty glass.

Liv set the bottle on the countertop and strode around the bar to sit next to Stefan.

"As I was saying, I asked myself what you'd do in my situation," Stefan continued. "That was when I came up with the idea of proving to the elves that they needed the House of Seven. So I've decided to take out their most wanted, thereby earning their favor."

Liv took a swig of her drink. "Not a bad approach. Although I might have just explained to them that I'd protect them from their nemeses rather than gone out and hunted them all down."

"Yeah, good point," Stefan stated. "But they'd probably believe you, since you've got that kind of reputation. I thought I should prove my loyalty, and now I only have two or three more villains to take down before I earn the High Council's respect."

"Then you'll ask them to sign the negotiation?" Liv asked.

"Yes, and I assume they will. Spincoster has been a huge pain in their asses," Stefan explained as his facial features shifted. "You really thought he was attractive?"

Liv glanced at the dead elf sprawled out behind them. "He's got pretty eyes, good bone structure and a nice ass."

"It isn't just about looks. Can he hold a delightful

conversation over drinks?" Stefan held up his whiskey, an expectant look in his eyes.

"Thanks to you, I'll never know," she said, clinking her glass against his.

"You're welcome." He glanced around, a peaceful expression on his face. "So what brings you and your chicken to Las Vegas?"

"Father Time wanted me to turn the chicken back into a scientist, but in order to do that, I have to track down this fae named Foggerbottom. However, he's not going to help me unless King Dumbface makes him, so I came here to get a decree from Rudolf, but now I have to be the best man at his wedding, which if he keeps up his antics might also double as his funeral," Liv said in one long sentence without taking a breath.

Stefan's blue eyes dazzled with amusement. "You really are a master of storytelling, Warrior Beaufont."

"Oh, where are my manners?" Liv asked, diving halfway over the bar and grabbing a tumbler. She sat it down in front of the chicken and poured her a drink. The chicken sniffed it before taking a small sip.

"And now you're having a drink with a bird while over-looking the Las Vegas Strip," Stefan said. "Seriously, how do your days not all run together from the monotony?"

Liv took a sip. "The whiskey helps."

Stefan leaned forward, whispering into Liv's ear. "Is it just me, or is your chicken looking at me strangely?"

Scientist had nearly finished the whiskey, which was definitely going to go straight to the bird's small head. She was in fact regarding Stefan with a weird expression. She almost appeared to be flirting as she blinked rapidly at him.

"She's not really my chicken," Liv explained. "I'm sort of just her protector. But soon I'll get her changed into whatever she is, and then she'll lead me to Shitkphace."

"I like to make up names for the bad guys I go after too," Stefan related. "I called Spincoster by a few different choice words while tracking him."

"That's the villain's real name," Liv corrected.

"Oh, your cases are far more interesting than mine," Stefan said, leaning away from the chicken when she neared him on the bar.

"Don't worry, she's just a bird," Liv consoled. "I'm mean, she's a scientist in the body of a bird, and apparently she can make crazy-awesome magic tech that defies time, but still, I'll protect you if she comes any closer."

The alcohol was apparently in full effect on the chicken. She set her head down on the bar, closing her eyes immediately.

Stefan sighed in relief. "Thanks. I sleep better at night knowing you've got my back."

When they'd been silent for a long moment, Stefan held up his glass. "So, looks like I finally got you to have that drink with me."

Liv glanced around at the empty rooftop. "Yes. It wasn't how I expected, but it totally works."

"And this wedding you have to attend…"

Liv gave him a skeptical expression. "What about it?"

"Will you need a date?" he asked.

Liv swallowed the rest of her drink, feeling her stomach warm. "I think we both know you phrased that sentence completely wrong."

Stefan blinked at her, confused. "Will you need someone to accompany you?" he tried again.

"I don't need anyone tagging along with me ever, Warrior Ludwig," she said at once.

He nodded, realizing his mistake. "Right. Of course. But if you find yourself wanting a partner in crime for the lavish affair, I would consider attending as your guest."

Liv was about to open her mouth to protest when Stefan held up his hand to pause her. "But please note that I'll mouth off to every fae who stands too close, subtly make fun of the king with jokes that soar over his head, and in so many words, encourage his bride to never breed with him."

Damn it to hell, Liv thought, narrowing her eyes at the man before her.

"What? Did I say something wrong?" Stefan asked, worry springing to his features.

She shook her head. "No, just the opposite. Wash your hands, and you can go to the wedding with me."

He winked. "You've got yourself a date."

CHAPTER TWENTY

By the time Papa Creola ponied up the information on where to find Foggerbottom, the chicken had passed out and she and Stefan had finished two bottles of high-end whiskey.

"It's about damn time," she'd replied to Father Time.

"Timing is everything, actually," the gnome replied.

"I have the decree. I don't have to worry about timing my request to Foggerbottom."

"I was referring to the events that happened on the rooftop in Las Vegas," Papa Creola stated.

Liv scowled at the screen. Of course, that gnome knew what had happened at the bar with the elf and Stefan. He seemed to have his hand in a lot of things.

"So you delayed sending me Foggerbottom's location so I could almost get killed by an elf?" Liv asked, the whiskey making her feel a bit sassier than usual. That probably wasn't a good thing since she was texting with a pretty important man. Maybe the most important man on Earth.

"No, I delayed so that you could be saved," he replied.

"You're meddling in affairs that don't involve you."

Papa Creola's reply came immediately. "EVERYTHING INVOLVES ME."

Liv sighed. Now wasn't the time to tell her new boss that he was coming across like an overbearing dictator.

Another message came through as she considered sending this message. "Phillippe Foggerbottom is on break, but will be at his post in six minutes and thirty-four seconds."

"Can you be more specific?" Liv asked, giggling to herself.

When Father Time didn't respond to what she had thought was a delightful joke, Liv created the portal, double-checking the location he'd given her for Foggerbottom. She wasn't drunk, but stepping through the portal into the airport in Frankfurt, Germany felt a bit like walking on the deck of a boat. She glanced down to ensure that the floor wasn't moving under her feet.

No, the tiled floor in the busy airport was still, although the people jostling by were moving like waves in the ocean.

Glancing around, Liv looked for signs to direct her. Thankfully, she didn't have to take a flight to find this Foggerbottom, but where she had to venture in the airport was almost more unpleasant than sitting next to some bloke who thought he owned the armrest between them on a plane.

Since Liv had time to spare, she stopped by the restroom. For a full minute, she stared around the stall, trying to decide what to do with the sleeping chicken. Setting it on the dirty airport bathroom floor seemed wrong, and that was when Liv noticed the changing table.

She wasn't sure what was worse, putting the chicken on the floor or a surface where babies have their butts wiped.

Once she was done with her business, she was unsurprised to find that the chicken hadn't woken up. She left it on the changing table while she washed her hands, which wasn't the most straightforward process in the world. The automatic soap dispenser didn't want to work until she pulled her hand back, thinking it was empty. Then it spat soap all over the countertop. She ended up using magic to make the dispenser work correctly. "You're welcome, Frankfurt airport," Liv said to herself as she tried to figure out how the blower worked. She kept running her hand over the sensors, wondering what she was missing.

A woman entered with a toddler in tow just as the blower blew lukewarm air into Liv's face, not at all in the direction of her hands. She zapped it, fixing the device so that it worked more efficiently.

"*Hier ist ein Huhn drin!*" the woman yelled from the stall Liv had just abandoned.

Although Liv didn't speak German, she was pretty sure the lady was screaming about the chicken. "Oh, sorry. That's my bird," she said in a rush, dashing through the open stall and grabbing Scientist.

The woman didn't appear amused as Liv backed away, lifting the chicken's clawed foot and making it wave at her and the toddler.

"Some people can't take a joke," Liv related to the sleeping bird.

The line for the Customs for non-German citizens was extraordinarily long, snaking through a giant room filled with irritable security guards. Liv stood on her tiptoes, trying to search for her guy. Right on cue, Phillippe Foggerbottom took the desk at the line for German citizens, which had zero people in it.

"Easy-peasy," Liv said, striding past all the grumpy tourists and making her way to the Customs agent, who was reviewing some documents in front of him.

"Mr. Foggerbottom," Liv said, noticing that the Customs agent was an attractive fae like most, with his dark hair and strong features. His wings were, of course, glamoured so no one could see them. His personality must have been too as he stared at the report.

"German passport," he said without glancing up.

"I'm actually a United States citizen," Liv said as others watched her with curiosity.

He huffed. "Then you go over to the line there." Foggerbottom pointed to the mile-long line beside them.

"Yes, but I'm actually in a hurry and need your help," Liv explained.

"So you cut the line, did you?"

Liv glanced behind her. "Well, there isn't anyone in this line presently."

"But did you ask all those in the other line if you could bypass them to get into a line where you don't belong?" Foggerbottom asked.

"I guess I can delay my mission to save the space-time continuum and go do that real quickly," Liv said, her tone laden with sarcasm.

Not picking up on her humor, Foggerbottom nodded, pulling his report up to cover his face. "Yes, do that."

Liv expected the fae to laugh and tell her he was kidding. When he didn't, she cleared her throat to get his attention. "Mr. Foggerbottom, I'm here because I need your help."

"German passport," he said firmly.

"Again, I don't have one," Liv replied.

"Do you have anything to declare? Fruit, vegetables, or livestock?"

Liv held up Scientist. "Yeah, I have a chicken."

"Custom forms," Foggerbottom stated.

"Again, I don't have them. What I do have is a decree from King Rudolfus Sweetwater stating that you must do what I request of you." Liv set the parchment down on the desk.

Slowly, irritation overflowing in the movement, Foggerbottom lowered the report, staring up at Liv for the first time. "What did you say?"

"I'm a magician, and I'm aware you're a fae," Liv began. "What I can't figure out is why you work in Customs here."

"I wanted a change of pace," Foggerbottom said coolly. "Something normal."

"How is this normal?" Liv asked, staring at the long line of angry travelers.

Slamming the report down, Foggerbottom scowled. "What is it that you want from me?"

Liv held up Scientist. "Remember when I said I had a chicken?"

"No," he answered.

"Okay, well, I have this chicken, which actually isn't one at all."

He nodded. "Clearly. It's an Italian woman by the name of Alicia."

"Alicia!" Liv exclaimed. However, to her disappointment, the bird didn't rouse. The whiskey had really knocked her out. Many of the tourists in the other line glared at Liv. "Anyway, I need you to change Alicia into her real form."

"And this decree you say was issued by my king?" Foggerbottom asked.

Liv pointed at the paper on the desk.

Like he had all the time in the world, Foggerbottom picked it up, unrolling it slowly. "Thing is, I'm sort in a hurry."

"Shush, I'm reading," the fae said tersely.

"I get that," Liv began. "But remember what I said about trying to save the space-time continuum?"

"I don't, actually."

"Anyway, if you could just zap this bird, returning her to normal, I'll be out of here, and you can go back to doing…" Staring around at the empty line, Liv shrugged. "Well, whatever it is you do here."

"I can't just turn Alicia here," Foggerbottom said, offense in his voice. "Does she even have her passport?"

"Well, since she's in chicken form, I'm going to guess no," Liv stated.

"Ms…"

"Beaufont," Liv supplied.

"Ms. Beaufont, this is a secure border for the German government," Foggerbottom said, an air of entitlement in his voice. "I can't allow you over this border without the proper paperwork, not to mention that you're in the wrong line entirely."

"Right," Liv said, drawing out the word. "I actually don't

need to cross through Customs. I'll just portal to wherever I need to go."

He huffed. "Which was always the problem with portaling. Anyone can go anywhere. There are no checks."

"Again, I'm trying to stop an issue regarding holes in the fabric of time. So if you're looking for a cause to be up in arms about, how about that one?"

Foggerbottom spread the decree on the desk. "I try not to get involved in magicians' business. It always comes back to haunt me."

"Which is why you're working in the mortal world in a place no magical creature would venture," Liv guessed.

"Not until today," Foggerbottom growled.

Liv held up the chicken. "So, Alicia. Will you please change her as your king requested?"

"Of course," Foggerbottom replied. "As soon as my lunch break comes around."

"What?" Liv nearly yelled. "But Rudolf said you had to do it."

"That's correct," the fae stated proudly. "However, he didn't specify *when* I needed to do it. And I'm not to attend to non-Customs business when I'm on the clock."

"Seriously?" Liv threw her arm wide. "There's no one else in line!"

"That could change at any moment," he fired back.

For effect, Liv stared off, tilting her head to the side. After a long minute, she looked back at the fae. "There still isn't anyone here."

"Are you not going to leave until I transform Alicia?" Foggerbottom asked.

"Are you just getting that impression?"

He let out a long breath. "Fine, but you can't do it here. It will draw too much attention. You must do it somewhere else." Holding out his hand, he tapped his palm with his fingertip. A loud boom sounded when a small pill appeared in his hand, followed by a plume of smoke.

"You're worried about *me* drawing too much attention?" Liv asked, but to her surprise, none of the mortals in line seemed to have noticed. They all were busy on their phones or regarding the ceiling with great attentiveness as they continued to wait.

"Take Alicia to a private place and have her swallow this," Foggerbottom ordered. "And you might want to cover her since she'll probably not be wearing clothes when she transforms."

Liv grabbed the pill, but just before she had it, Foggerbottom closed his fingers over it. "One more thing. Don't portal with this, or it will negate its effects."

Liv glanced around. "Where exactly do you propose I go to transform her, then?"

The fae opened his fingers, dropping the pill on his desk. "That's not my problem."

CHAPTER TWENTY-ONE

"I think Mr. Foggerbottom should seriously work on his customer service skills," Liv said to Alicia, who was still fast asleep. She'd returned to the bathroom, which now had a working soap dispenser and dryer. The women in line gave her a strange expression, as if speaking to a sleeping chicken was weird.

Liv held up the bird. "She's my service chicken. I can't find my way through the airport without her."

Some of the women seemed to buy this excuse. The others continued to eye Liv like she was deranged.

"Hey, Alicia, I need you to wake up," Liv said, noticing that this sharpened the attention of those in line.

"Because I need to make it to my gate," Liv stated, talking to the eavesdropping women.

Shaking the bird slightly, Liv tried to rouse her. That didn't work. She stuck her hand under the faucet, getting it wet before running it over the chicken's feathers. Nothing worked. It occurred to Liv that she'd recently learned a spell that could do the trick.

She pointed at the chicken and muttered an incantation. Like a rooster waking at dawn, Alicia let out a loud squawk, making everyone in the bathroom cover their ears as the noise echoed off the tiled walls.

"There you are!" Liv exclaimed. "I know that your name is Alicia, and I have what you need to…"

She noticed the queue of ladies snooping on her and backed into a corner, covering her mouth. "I have what you need to transform into a person."

The chicken still appeared disoriented but perked up at this news. However, Liv noticed that the line for the stalls had gotten longer since she'd entered.

"Oh, crud," Liv stated, turning her attention to the women. "I'm sorry to ask this, but my chicken really needs to use the restroom. She's not good at holding it because her bladder is even smaller than her brain."

Alicia squawked in protest.

Liv whispered, "Hey, just go with it."

Returning her attention to the women, Liv asked, "Can she please cut in line? I promise she won't be long."

The woman at the front smiled sensitively at Liv. "Yes, go on, dear. I think it's sweet that you chose a chicken as your companion."

"Thanks," Liv said, taking off for the first open stall. She set Alicia down on the floor and put the pill on a clean tissue in front of her. "See, I care. I'm not having you eat off the bathroom floor. You need to swallow that pill, and then you'll transform. Got it?"

The bird nodded.

Liv was about to close the stall door to give Alicia privacy when she remembered what Foggerbottom had said. She slipped off her cloak and hung it up on the stall, giving the chicken one last look. "Here, this is for when you're back to normal. We'll get you shoes and whatever else once I know what size you are."

The chicken blinked appreciatively at her as she closed the stall door.

"I'll just be out here waiting until you're done," Liv said, noticing that the ladies in the line were still watching with curiosity.

She smiled meekly at them. "My chicken likes privacy when doing her business."

"As she should," the woman who had allowed her to cut in line said.

A moment later there was a loud popping noise, making everyone in the bathroom but Liv jump. She was way too used to strange, loud noises as of late.

There was a brush of fabric, and the stall door attempted to open into Liv. She backed up as an attractive woman with long, silky brown hair and full lips stepped out of the stall.

Every woman in line gaped in disbelief at Alicia as she marched barefoot to the sink to wash her hands.

Liv was tense, wondering how she'd cover this. Alicia gave Liv an appreciative look as she dried her hands. "Thanks for...well, you know," she said in a thick Italian accent.

The ladies all swiveled their heads to Liv, waiting for her response. "You're welcome. I'm glad you're feeling better after all that."

"Yes, and now I could use some food," Alicia said with a wink. "I'm feeling a bit peckish."

CHAPTER TWENTY-TWO

Liv and Alicia giggled for a solid minute over the bathroom scene as they picked out clothes for her at a nearby outlet store.

The women in the bathroom had probably forgotten about what had happened as soon as the two magicians exited. That was the great thing about mortals. They forgot that which they couldn't explain, which wasn't fair to them, Liv knew. Soon she'd return to her mission of freeing them from the curse that kept them from seeing magic.

"Peckish," Liv said with a laugh. "That was a good one."

Alicia held up a pair of jeans, eyeing them. "Yes, your bad puns have rubbed off on me."

"I guessed they would. We spent a lot of time together." Liv held up a pair of flats.

Alicia nodded, taking them along with the other clothes she'd picked out. She disappeared behind a changing wall. "Yes, we did. You live a very interesting life, Warrior Beaufont."

"It's far more chaotic than it used to be," Liv stated. "I used to work in a repair shop full-time, tinkering with devices."

The black cape Liv had given Alicia draped over the top of the wall. "Oh, well, then you'll love *my* shop."

"You have a repair shop?"

"No, it's more of a magical-tech place. Well, at least it used to be."

"Before Shitface turned you into a chicken?" Liv asked.

"Yes. At first, he posed as a normal customer who needed custom stuff made," Alicia explained. "But before I knew it, I was being held hostage by these gremlins. I didn't want to make the devices he asked of me. They all messed with time. Rewound events or paused them or sped them up."

"Giving Papa Creola a huge headache," Liv related.

"I didn't have a choice, though," Alicia went on. "He told me he was going to kill me, so I did what he wanted, thinking that he'd go away. However, just when I thought I was done with him, he turned me into a chicken. One minute I'm in my shop trying to figure out what's going on, and then he teleports me to that barbeque place. That wasn't enough for Shitkphace, though. He hadn't figured out how to replicate my work."

"Which was why time kept getting messed up at Liam's restaurant," Liv guessed.

"Exactly," Alicia affirmed. "So Shitkphace came and got me and promised to turn me back and leave me alone if I created blueprints for him."

Liv lowered her chin. "And you believed the scoundrel?"

"Believe me, I feel like an idiot," Alicia stated, angst in her voice. "But I didn't really have a choice. I made the blueprints for him so he could replicate my work, and just when I thought he was going to turn me back, he sent me to you. All of a sudden, I was on a beach with a magician from the House of Seven and a giant. It was insane."

"Yes, I think he wanted his gremlin back," Liv related, remembering the events in Seattle.

"But it's all worked out in the end," Alicia said, coming out from behind the wall wearing a paisley top and jeans. Her beauty was breathtaking.

Liv held up a feathered headband. "For your hair?"

Alicia scowled back at her.

"What? Is it too soon?" Liv jested.

"Can we get something to eat? I'm starving."

"Yeah, what do you want? Chicken tenders? Chicken pot pie? Chicken salad?"

The frown on Alicia's face deepened.

Liv slapped her hand to her forehead. "I'm sorry. I forgot you're Italian. How about chicken marsala? Or chicken piccata?"

Alicia stormed off, her long brown hair jerking back and forth.

"Oh, or chicken cacciatore?"

"You're not funny, Liv," Alicia said when she caught up with her after paying for the clothes.

"Then why are you smiling?" Liv asked, spying the grin the former chicken was trying to hide.

Alicia allowed herself to laugh fully. "Okay, you are. I swear, I would have lost my mind if it wasn't for you. The way you make fun of sweet Rory is really entertaining. He's such a lovely man."

"Yes, he is," Liv said, then thought of something. "You don't by chance know what he does for a living, do you?"

Alicia thought for a moment. "No, I never saw any clues. He was always so busy trying to feed me."

Liv nodded. "Yes, he's like a grandmother that way."

"And then there was King Rudolf," Alicia said. "He's one of the most attractive men I've ever seen."

"Which just proves that looks can take a person to big places."

"Oh, but the most beautiful man I've ever seen was the one on the rooftop in Las Vegas," Alicia said.

"Oh, Spincoster?" Liv asked. "Yeah, he was sort of hot for an elf, although I could never get over the pointy ears and hippie lifestyle."

"No, I meant your friend Stefan," Alicia said when they came to the food court in the airport.

"Is he?" Liv asked. "I hadn't really noticed."

"Of course, you have," Alicia said, getting in line at a pizza restaurant.

"Seriously, you're going to have pizza in Germany?" Liv asked.

"I'm starving," Alicia said. "I don't care if it's not even that good. Pizza tastes like home for me."

"Yes, I'm sure you miss it," Liv related. "Where is home? Rome?"

Alicia shook her head. "Actually, my shop is in Venice. It doesn't have the best pizza in Italy, but I like it just fine."

"Why is that? I thought the Venetians were the best at everything?" Liv asked.

"We are," Alicia said smugly. "But we don't have pizza ovens."

"Oh, because burning down the island would be a pretty bad deal," Liv guessed.

"That's right," Alicia affirmed.

"So Shitface is in Venice still?"

A seething expression crossed Alicia's face. "Yes, he's probably still in my shop."

"Which means he'll be easy to find."

"Yes, but you have to be careful," Alicia stated. "He's a very powerful magician, and he has a ton of magical tech devices, so his store of energy will outlast yours. Then there are his repugnant gremlins."

Liv thought for a moment. "Sounds like we need to outsmart him." She smiled at the scientist. "I think you and I will make a great team for this project."

CHAPTER TWENTY-THREE

Liv watched from the roof of the building across from Alicia's shop. The store appeared to sell things like phone batteries and chargers to tourists. However, behind a faux wall, those who were in the know could browse a large collection of magical-tech devices. Alicia made and sold phones with universal contact lists. All the user had to do was think of the person they wanted to message and the number automatically dialed whether they had it or not. There were also self-typing computers, which apparently a lot of writers used, according to Alicia. They simply thought out the story and the computer did the rest. And then there were instant hair dryers, unlimited storage jump drives, and iceless ice chests that were always cold without a source.

Liv couldn't wait to explore the shop. She could learn a thing or two from Alicia. But first, she had to get rid of the infestation that had taken over the shop.

The streets of Venice were quiet as the sun rose over the canal. However, soon the many alleyways would be buzzing with tourists who would eye the fresh-made pasta in the display windows with delight. Liv had never been to a place so rich in history and culture. She had soon discovered from talking to Alicia that the Venetians were loving and open people who also held a great deal of pride. There were things only the Venetians could do, like blow glass or repair the gondolas.

Liv watched as Alicia laid down a piece of dark chocolate on the cobbled street. She was in disguise, wearing one of the intricately decorated masks Venice was known for.

"You've grown to like her," Plato said, arriving by her side and peering over the edge of the building.

"Yes, and I'll miss my little chicken, but you must never tell anyone that."

"I think we both know I'm not telling anyone anything, but if you think it's a secret that you have a heart, well, I hate to be the bearer of bad news."

Liv frowned. "Do you think people suspect?"

"I think they might not buy your snarky, heartless act."

"Well, what can I do?" Liv asked, a pleading in her voice.

"Kick a kitten," Plato suggested.

Liv gave him one long, repulsed look.

"Okay, fine," he surrendered. "You don't have to *kick* the kitten. Maybe just insult it. Make fun of it for being short and inexperienced."

Liv continued to regard the lynx like he'd gone too far, although she knew he'd never hurt an innocent animal...or at least she hoped. She didn't know much...well, really anything about the feline beside her. Only that she loved him almost more than anyone else. He was...well, the best way she knew how to put it was that Plato was a part of her.

"What's your deal with kittens?" Liv asked him.

He shrugged. "I only have a few kryptonites in this world."

"What about in other worlds?" Liv asked, trying not to get excited that the lynx was sharing with her. She maintained an indifferent stance, causally staring over the edge of the building as Alicia continued to lay the bait.

"Still only a few," he answered.

"So we know that you're powerless against lophos," Liv said, thinking about when they had encountered the ancient snake in the monastery.

Plato watched as Alicia disappeared behind a bend. The door to the shop opened and three gremlins peeked their heads out, each looking in a different direction as they sniffed the air.

"And then you mentioned something about how sharing your secrets would cause you to lose your power," Liv continued.

"I don't believe I did mention that," Plato said as the gremlins piled out of the shop, hitting each other as they raced for the chocolate. Alicia had shared that Shitkphace didn't feed the gremlins very well, instead forcing them to scavenge for food. That made their strategy planning a bit easier for the first phase.

"Well, maybe I deduced that," Liv stated. "And then it appears on the short list of your shortcomings are kittens. That makes total sense. An all-powerful being who can go anywhere and transform into many different things is disempowered by sweet little cuddly kittens."

"They poop in a box and chase their tails," Plato argued.

"Right, which only further proves my point about how incredibly strange it is to have a kryptonite that is so unsuspecting," Liv said.

When Plato didn't appear interested in adding to her observations, she shrugged. "But I guess the snake was pretty powerful. And then there are secrets. That's everyone's shortcoming, isn't it?"

"I'm not certain," Plato said. "I can't speak for everyone. However, if we're going to stay on schedule, I better be going."

Liv nodded, watching as the gremlins took the bait. "Thanks for helping rid us of those nuisances."

Plato gave her a casual glance over his shoulder as he disappeared.

"I simply hope you don't meet a kitten tonight. Or on any night," Liv said to the cold dawn air. "I hope you never meet your kryptonite, Plato."

CHAPTER TWENTY-FOUR

The first step in Alicia and Liv's complex plan was to draw the gremlins away from the shop. They were, as Liv knew from her first encounter with them, tricky, slippery little jerks. According to Alicia, they were ruthless, taking cheap shots and doing despicable things. Liv laughed to herself, realizing they'd meet their match with Plato.

The next part of the plan involved drawing Shitkphace away from the shop, which would be slightly more difficult. He apparently didn't leave it that often, usually sending the gremlins out to do his bidding. But if they had sunk to the bottom of the canal, or whatever Plato decided to do with them, they couldn't run errands for the evil magician.

However, Liv knew they couldn't simply draw Shitkphace away. They had to weaken him first. She could spar with him for hours, but that would only diminish her magical reserves. No, to reduce an evil, power-hungry magician's magical energy, they needed to rely on what they knew about him.

According to Alicia, he was a workaholic, obsessed with his deadlines, pushing himself to work long hours, and in the past, pushing Alicia to produce the magical tech.

Liv waited until she saw the sparks fly from the back of the building to the shop. The lights in the shop flickered before all the windows went completely dark.

Alicia had done both her jobs. Now it was Liv's turn. She stepped onto the ledge of the two-story building where she stood. Taking a deep breath, she launched into the air, landing in a crouch in front of the dark shop. Liv flipped up her head, staring straight at the door in front of her.

It was almost showtime.

Alicia De Luca had lived in Venice for a long time. She knew this island better than most, although for even the locals it was a maze at times. For that reason, she wanted to be the one who drew Shitkphace away. It only made sense. However, she was also the only one who could build the electromagnetic signal.

She'd advised Liv Beaufont as best as she could, giving her a strategy for getting around through the canals. Alicia had spent enough time with the magician to know that she could adapt and figure things out on her own, but Shitkphace wasn't like others. He'd be armed, and he'd be out for vengeance—especially when he realized he'd been tricked. And if he paused things, Liv would be screwed. And it would be all Alicia's fault.

She waited in the shadows behind her shop. Strangely, she could smell the familiarity of the place at her back. It had been her parents' shop before she'd inherited it. They had sold potions and herbs to the local magical community. Although supportive of Alicia, they hadn't understood her obsession with tinkering.

Magical tech wasn't just strange in the old world, where things were done a different way. It was still considered pretty adventuresome in circles of progressive magicians. That was why when the House of Seven had moved to registering magicians who used technology. It was considered extremely liberal.

When it was time for Alicia's parents to retire, she took over the shop, phasing out the potions and replacing them with the magical tech she created. Venetians hadn't known how to respond to the progressive move at first. However, within the first year, her shop was busy all the time, overwhelmed with orders. That kind of attention brought in magicians and magical creatures from all over. Everything was going great until Shitkphace showed up on a windy autumn day. From that moment on, Alicia had regretted altering her parent's shop and bringing this evil to their home.

"*Questo è per voi Mamma e Papà*," Alicia said, looking out at the starry sky from between the buildings.

A moment later, the back door of the shop swung open, which made Alicia tense and zip up her body against the stucco wall behind her. Water sloshed over her galoshes. The tide was rising. They didn't have long.

"Damn it!" Shitkphace said, his nasal tone grating

against Alicia's core. She hadn't missed that voice. "What happened to the electricity?"

I happened to it, you big faced jerk, Alicia thought, holding her breath.

"How am I supposed to..." Shitkphace muttered to himself.

There was no way to fix the generator manually, not the way that Alicia had damaged it. She'd have to buy a brand new one after this, but it would be worth it. She was also going to buy herself a new set of tools and a cat, and innovate a better security system.

A popping noise told her that Shitkphace had done the only thing available to him to fix the problem—he'd relied on his magic to fix the generator. That would cost him half his reserves, if not more.

He sighed and cursed loudly as he slammed the back door.

Alicia rolled her eyes, hoping he hadn't broken anything in her shop by slamming things around.

I'll also have the whole place deep-cleaned once he's out.

She eyed her watch, counting the seconds until the next phase. Soon she'd be back in her shop, where she belonged. Nothing had ever sounded so good.

Gremlins were pretty much the most annoying creatures on the Earth. For no one else on this planet would Plato face such horrid beasts, but no one was like Olivia Beaufont. She was every bit as incredible as her parents had told him on that day so many years ago. What astonished Plato was that he hadn't believed Guinevere and Theodore Beaufont when they'd told him about their daughter. He'd thought they were biased, overprotective parents. Instead of believing what they told him about Olivia, Plato'd had to learn it on his own, but it was almost better that way.

The gremlins squeaked and cackled as they ran through the streets of Venice. Plato lifted his head from the dead-end of the dark alley, his tiger eyes glowing yellow. Seeing perfectly in the dark, he watched as the three gremlins froze at the sight of the giant cat. They screamed, running backward and dropping many of the chocolates they'd collected.

Plato lowered his head, shaking it. This was almost too easy.

He vanished, appearing in the place he knew the gremlins would turn down next. They were incredibly easy to predict. All he had to do was think of the short-term solution. That was what gremlins did.

The gremlins' eyes widened at the sight of the black panther. One looked to have wet himself, but that could just be from the water they were splashing through. Soon the streets of Venice would be flooded. Plato would have run these pests to the far side of the island by then, where they'd take a boat to get as far from him as they could, never returning again.

He disappeared, waiting for the gremlins to turn the corner. It would take them a bit longer this time because they were on edge, sneaking around the corners instead of running around wildly. It didn't take much to diminish their morale.

The gremlins were the opposite of Liv. Nothing ever

broke the girl. Plato had met her five years ago as Olivia Beaufont and had soon learned exactly why her parents had wanted him to watch out for her if anything should ever happen to them. She was everything they had said: passionate, intelligent, and absolutely meant for greatness.

Whether Guinevere and Theodore Beaufont subscribed to the prophecies that could involve their children, Plato would never know. All he knew for sure was that a decade prior, those two magicians had asked one favor of him in repayment for something they had done to help him. He had spent several years babysitting magicians and other magical creatures out of obligation, and that was what he'd thought he was getting into again when he'd agreed to watch over Olivia if something should ever happen to them.

Plato was a lot of things, but he was always true to his word. That was why when Guinevere and Theodore Beaufont died, he dutifully showed up beside Liv. However, the agreement was only that he protect her until she came to full power, and that time had long since passed, once she became a Warrior for the House of Seven.

Plato had originally agreed to watch over Olivia Beaufont out of obligation. However, he planned to stay by Liv's side for as long as she let him because she was the most incredible person he'd met in his long life.

He only hoped she never found out all his secrets. Some she might not forgive him for. Such was the way of a lynx.

CHAPTER TWENTY-FIVE

The water in the streets was almost to Liv's ankles. She sloshed through it, noticing how the water slowed her down.

This is going to make for an interesting chase, she thought as she neared the door. The lights had just flickered back to life in the tech shop. She ran through what Alicia had told her about Shitkphace in her head. He was a conniving liar who also happened to be highly superstitious. Even more important than that was the fact that he was highly regimented.

When he had taken over her shop, he'd reorganized it, putting things where he thought they should go. Liv was counting on this for the next phase. This plan was all about being smarter and more strategic than Shitkphace, which for two ladies like Alicia and Liv that shouldn't have been hard.

Raising her hand, Liv took a deep breath before rapping on the door.

"Go away!" Shitkphace yelled.

Liv knocked again.

"I said, go away!"

Another knock, this one louder.

"Klutz, go get that!" Shitkphace ordered.

Knock, knock.

"Klutz? Ponny? Ding?" Shitkphace yelled. "Where are you worthless thwarts?"

Knock, knock.

"Damn it!" Shitkphace yelled, whipping the door back. The lower half stayed in place, keeping the water flooding the streets from entering the shop.

Liv peeked out from under her hood as if it was pouring rain. "Hey, there. Sorry to bother you, but I just lost power in my flat." She pointed roughly over her shoulder.

"I don't care!" Shitkphace had a long gray goatee and a head full of dreadlocks that fell past his shoulders.

"I think gremlins took out the power," Liv said. "I didn't realize we had an infestation here. I just wanted to see—"

"I'm busy!" Shitkphace sputtered, spitting on Liv.

"Oh, sorry," she said, glancing over her shoulder, looking for the object Alicia had told her about. "Still, I don't think that will keep you from getting your place searched."

"Searched?" Shitkphace said, his tone suddenly edgy.

"Oh, yes," Liv stated. "I reported the gremlins to the House of Seven, since I'm sure they aren't registered, and you know how that organization gets about such things. They are sending over a Warrior right now."

"A Warrior?" Shitkphace peeked out his head, looking both ways up and down the narrow alley.

"Yes. I heard they were sending over Decar Sinclair," Liv stated, catching a glimpse of the object she was looking for—a wind-up pink flamingo. When it was wound up, it shuffled forward on its feet, and what was important about the seemingly simple toy was that it was Shitkphace's most treasured item. That's why it was sitting on a top shelf at the back of the front room, exactly where Alicia had said.

"Not Decar Sinclair," Shitkphace said in a hushed voice.

She nodded, trying to quell her frustration over this man being scared of the other Warrior. "Yes, and I hear he will be using deadly force."

Just as Alicia had foretold, Shitkphace slipped his hand into the pocket of his robe.

So he was *armed.*

"Good to know," Shitkphace said, again glancing up and down the alley.

While he was distracted, Liv flicked her finger at the small pink toy. It disappeared and reappeared in her hand, her fingers closing around it.

"Well, good luck with Decar," Liv said, backing away, the water's current nearly making her trip.

"Yeah, I hope you're wrong, and they send a different Warrior," Shitkphace said, his shoulders growing tense as he studied the area.

When she was a safe distance away, Liv opened her fingers, allowing him a glimpse of the object she'd just stolen. The pink winked out from her hand, catching Shitkphace's gaze at once.

He spun around to look at the shelf and then back around. "Give that back!"

Liv shook her head. "If you want your little trinket

back, you'll have to catch me!" She took off running, knowing she didn't have long before Shitkphace was after her.

Using a spying device she had constructed when they returned to Venice, Alicia had overheard Liv's conversation with Shitkphace and knew the chase was on.

She slid out of the dark and over to the back door to the shop. Shaking her head, she laughed to herself. Shitkphace was scared of Decar Sinclair, but he didn't know a thing about Liv Beaufont. He was about to learn that he should fear her.

Alicia slid the unlocker into the side of the backdoor. Shitkphace had wards on the shop, but they'd come down the moment he'd used his power reserves to turn the electricity back on. Most still wouldn't be able to break into the shop because of the security that Alicia had installed on the building. However, if anyone knew how to get around those systems, it was the person who had invented them.

The magic-tech buzzed in Alicia's hand as the lock released. She pushed open the backdoor of the shop, a wave of nostalgia washing over her. She was concerned about Liv, and whether she'd made it to the first barrier yet or in time. She didn't hear anything over the spyware. However, she knew she couldn't worry about Liv, and probably didn't need to. The Warrior would be fine—or she wouldn't, and she'd find a different way. All Alicia could do was what she had come to the shop for.

Without being in her shop, she'd been able to build the

unlocker, the spyware, and the barrier. However, what she needed to create the electromagnetic signal could only be found in this shop.

Alicia let out a deep breath, nearly choking up as she laid her eyes on the workstation where she'd done her best work. There had been a time when she'd thought she'd never return here, at least not in human form. Although she hadn't given up, it had been difficult to hold onto hope after everything Shitkphace had put her through. But she was here now, and that much closer to shutting down the evil magician for good.

From the dark corners of the shop, small mechanical noises sounded.

Alicia tensed.

They couldn't still be here. She was sure they were gone.

CHAPTER TWENTY-SIX

Splashing through the streets, Liv rounded the first corner, pulling the thick metal screen into place. It was attached to the brick wall of a building and drew across the alleyway like an accordion door.

She flexed her hand in front of her face.

It had to have worked. She remembered the last instance when the time remotes were used on her and she was rewound. Alicia said that sometimes when people were paused or fast-forwarded they remembered it, especially if they weren't mortals. However, sometimes they didn't remember anything, and then they experienced a little glitch in their movements, like a screen flickering. Liv didn't have any of that happening to her. She hadn't been paused or rewound.

Shitkphace would have tried to use the remote to stop her. When that didn't work, he'd almost certainly have come after her, but the flood barrier would slow him down. He'd have to hop over that and then charge after her.

Liv pressed her ear to the accordion barrier she'd helped Alicia to put up earlier that day. It was made out of simple tin, but it was enchanted with a time ward spell. Together the two combined to keep Liv safe from what Shitkphace could do with the remote. However, it wouldn't last, and it wasn't meant to.

A moment later, she heard splashing on the other side of the barrier. She was suddenly grateful for the rising water, which would make it easier to have Shitkphace follow her, although she was already soaked to the bone.

As she had practiced, Liv ran, kicking off the side of the building and grabbing the shutter on the opposite wall. She pulled herself up to the second story and continued climbing to the top as she heard the barrier being pushed out of the way.

"Damn it!" Shitkphace said from below. "This is Alicia De Luca's doing."

Liv managed to soundlessly climb all the way to the rooftop. From there, she spied Shitkphace kick the barrier. He really had a bad attitude, which was going to make this more fun.

"Hey, Shitface!" Liv yelled, holding up the pink flamingo. "Are you looking for this?"

He grimaced up at her, his eyes narrowed. "My name is Shitkphace."

"You say potato, I say Shitface," Liv said, smiling down at the magician.

He lifted his hand, holding a remote. "You'll pay for this."

"Not yet, I won't," Liv said, knowing she was far enough

away that the remote shouldn't be able to work. She and Alicia had tried to think of everything.

Shitkphace realized a moment later that it wasn't going to work.

"Oh, are you trying to pause me? Rewind me? Make me come back down?" Liv asked.

"I'm going to punish you!" Shitkphace declared.

"Cool, but first, you're going to have to catch me," Liv sang.

"Damn it to hell," Shitkphace said, then he rose off the ground.

Oh, hell. He's floating. No, flying. Whatever he's doing, it was making his climb up to the third story much faster than Liv's. She took off at a sprint, hoping to make the next station before he caught up with her.

Alicia choked back tears as the robotic panda and lion marched out of the shadows.

"Plotting Panda! Laidback Lion!" Alicia rejoiced, running over and dropping to her knees. "I thought Shitkphace had destroyed you!"

Like two puppies excited to be reunited with their owners, the little metal creatures pressed lovingly into Alicia as she pulled them into her arms. "I thought I'd never see you two again!"

"We hid," Laidback Lion said, pointing to the other robot when he was released. "It was his idea."

Alicia laughed, wiping away a tear brought on by the

unexpected surprise. "Plotting Panda, that was quick thinking."

He bowed slightly. "Thank you. And Laidback Lion kept me quiet while we hid from those gremlins."

"You two really are good for one another," Alicia stated, looking the robots over for any signs of wear and tear. They had been her first projects and were still her favorites. She'd created the robots from scratch, even painting the designs on their metal bodies, making Plotting Panda look like a cuddly bear, and Laidback Lion like a courageous cat. Unlike mortal robots, these could do more than menial tasks. They had been her right hands in the shop, helping her with every project.

"Are you okay, Dr. De Luca?" Laidback Lion asked.

She nodded. "But I've got to get straight to work on building an electromagnetic device that will broadcast a signal all over the island."

"But that will stop all magic-tech devices from working," Plotting Panda blurted, suddenly worried.

"I know," she said remorsefully. "Which means you two will be incapacitated. But once we get rid of Shitkphace, I'll turn off the device and bring you two back. I promise. Will you please help?"

Without hesitating, the two robots started forward.

"Absolutely!" Laidback Lion said. "Just tell us what you need done."

"I'll gather the supplies," Plotting Panda added.

Alicia smiled. Before, building the device for the signal in time was going to be cutting it close. Now, with her two best friends, she had a chance. She just hoped Liv held Shitkphace off long enough.

CHAPTER TWENTY-SEVEN

Of course, Shitface could fly, Liv lamented as she sped across the rooftop, water, from the last rain, flying into her face with each stomp of her boots.

Alicia had said he was incredibly powerful, using the magic-tech she'd created to hone his skills and add to his strength. Flying wasn't something she'd mentioned, though. Liv only hoped he'd further depleted his reserves with that little stunt.

"Stop where you are!" Shitkphace commanded.

Liv halted, peering over the edge of the building. According to the plan, she was supposed to have a little bit longer to scale back down the building. However, in that plan, Shitkphace was supposed to climb up after her, not fly.

"Do you know if your little wind-up toy is waterproof?" Liv asked, holding up the pink flamingo.

Shitkphace's eyes widened. "Don't throw it in the canal. Just tell me what you want!"

"Throw it in the canal?" Liv asked. "I wouldn't dream of

it." She took a step onto the ledge, really doubting if what she had in mind would work.

"Give it to me," Shitkphace ordered, taking a step toward her, his hand on the remote.

Liv was out of time. She had to take the plunge before he paused her. Figuratively. And literally.

"Like I said before, if you want it, come and get it." Liv took a casual step off the side of the building and plunged over the edge.

Plato was nearly at the end of his mission. Popping up in front of the gremlins at every other turn and unknown to them, getting them to follow the path he'd chosen, had been boringly easy.

The small-brained creatures were not only incredibly predictable, but their fearful reaction was always the same when they encountered a panther, a leopard, or whatever other form Plato decided to take.

Preparing for the last phase of the plan, Plato stared at the train station. The last transport of the night was about to head off, right on time. Three frightened gremlins who were being terrorized by a shapeshifting cat would jump that train in a second, desperately wanting to be as far from this haunted island as possible.

Plato heard the ragged breath of one of the creatures as he crouched in the shadows. One last show, and then he could swoop in to check on Liv. He didn't think she actually needed his help. She generally didn't. But he still preferred to keep an eye on her, just in case.

There *had* been the incidents on the Matterhorn and with the mermaid where he found himself useful for once. Liv probably would have gotten away in both instances without his intervention, but he had been happy to save her.

The truth was that she'd saved Plato a thousand times. Not from death, but from himself. From loneliness. From the monotony that went with being immortal.

He and Papa Creola understood each other better than anyone ever would. They both had incredible skills, the weight of the world resting on their shoulders and an unshakeable feeling that it would never ever be enough, no matter how hard they tried. Liv made those melancholy feelings disappear for Plato, or at least they receded.

When he was sure the gremlins were just around the corner, Plato sprang out in the form of a cheetah. He growled, his eyes glowing brightly.

As he expected, the two gremlins sprinted toward the train, not daring to look back.

Plato's victory was short lived as he scanned the alley.

There had been three gremlins… Which begged the question of where the third was.

Working with Plotting Panda and Laidback Lion again was just like old times. Seamlessly, they built the electromagnetic device together, Alicia supervising while the two robots did most of the work.

As usual, Plotting Panda was working furiously, soldering wires into place and checking the fit of the different joints. Meanwhile, Laidback Lion casually looked over the design, unhurried by the panda's never-ending excitement.

"How much longer until Shitkphace is back?" Plotting Panda asked.

Alicia eyed her watch. According to what she'd heard on the spyware last, Liv was on schedule, about to climb back down the other side of the building. It sounded as though everything was going according to plan. "We need to have this up and broadcasting a signal in less than two minutes."

"I think we can do it," Laidback Lion stated.

Plotting Panda grabbed a small wrench out of his hand. "Not if you don't work faster."

Alicia hid her smile. She'd created the two robots to complement each other. In actuality, they butted heads constantly, but still, the sentiment had worked. One kept her motivated while the other kept her balanced and relaxed.

They continued to work until the telltale sound of someone at the door made all three of them look up. The door handle jiggled, and there was a slight scratching on the wood. And then in the window, two ears appeared, followed by the face of a gremlin.

CHAPTER TWENTY-EIGHT

Liv's stomach jumped into her throat when she took the plunge over the side of the building, landing in the canal seconds later.

The water was cold and tasted of salt. Thankfully it smelled fresh, but still, she didn't plan on spending much time in the canal.

She glanced up as Shitkphace peered over the edge of the building.

Liv held up the pink flamingo, a teasing look in her eyes. "I've still got it. Let's hope it still works."

He pointed the remote at her, but she dove just in time, kicking hard and swimming in the direction of the Grand Canal. She'd have to get out of the water before then. Otherwise, swimming in the canal was about like playing in the streets at night. She'd risk getting mauled by a propeller if she wasn't careful.

When she was almost out of air, Liv came up to the surface. She caught sight of Shitkphace descending from the roof of the building as casually as if he were taking an elevator, his arms crossed over his chest and a madder-than-hell expression on his face. He hadn't spotted her yet, but from the way his eyes were scanning the water, he would soon.

Liv climbed onto the street, grateful that the rising tide made it easier. She was thoroughly soaked, but she was still alive. All she had to do was distract Shitkphace for another minute, and then she could take him down properly.

Once she was on her feet, Liv ran like hell down the closest alley. Shitkphace's head flipped up and he dropped to the pavement, pointing the remote at her.

Liv had to get to the next barrier in time, but it was at the far end of the alleyway and he was directly behind her. Too close.

He pointed the remote. Pressed a button. She froze.

"The gremlins!" Alicia said, fear in her voice.

Plotting Panda hurried over to the counter, using impressive acrobatic skills to jump back and forth between the walls until he arrived at the top. He peered through the window. "Just one," he corrected. "But he seems really mad."

"Yes, we sort of tricked them," Alicia stated. "Reinforce the door. We can't allow him in here."

Alicia'd had to take down the wards to get into her shop. Without those up, there was little to stop the conniving, slippery gremlin from getting back in. Then they'd have their hands full, and there'd be little hope of building the electromagnetic device in time.

"I think if I stand guard at the door, I can keep him out," Plotting Panda said.

"And I'll continue to help with the device," Laidback Lion said.

Alicia nodded, going back to work. However, she couldn't help but notice the grief-stricken expression on the panda's face. "What is it?"

"Nothing..." he lied. "At least, I don't think it's anything."

"What is the gremlin doing?" she asked, as she worked furiously.

"That's the thing," he said, craning his head to look to the side through the window. "He's disappeared."

CHAPTER TWENTY-NINE

Liv was frozen. Paralyzed. Her eyes didn't even blink. She could think in her head, but even that felt strangely delayed.

Alicia hadn't gotten the signal broadcasted yet. Things weren't going to plan now.

Angry footsteps splashed through the water as Shitkphace approached. He ripped the pink flamingo from Liv's hands, standing over her with an air of superiority.

"I don't know who you think you are, making me go after you, but you've messed with the wrong magician," he said, spittle flying out of his mouth and landing on Liv's face. He really needed to learn how to talk without drenching people in saliva.

Holding up the remote, he waved it in front of Liv's face. "Do you know what I can do with this, little girl?"

If he'd unpaused Liv, she could have answered. Apparently, it was a rhetorical question because he didn't grant her the opportunity to speak. "I can rewind you so we never meet. So you never annoy me with your presence." He dared to step in closer, breathing on her frozen face. "I can rewind you until you never exist. Would you like me to do that, little girl?"

Again, there was no answer from Liv. It was a totally one-sided conversation.

"Or how about I fast-forward you until you're old and gray? Would you like that?" Shitkphace asked.

Liv thought these questions sort of answered themselves. How many people would jump up and down and say, "Yes, please, erase my existence with a push of a button."

"Although it's fun fast-forwarding people until they are no more, it doesn't really have the same payoff as watching an enemy suffer," Shitkphace said. "One moment they are here, and then poof! They are a bag of bones on the floor. For that reason, I think I'll handle you differently than my last."

Liv didn't know what that meant for her, but she wasn't excited to find out.

Unfortunately for her, Shitkphace wasn't wasting any time all of a sudden. He pulled back his fist and launched it into her gut, making her nearly topple over from the assault she could neither stop nor defend herself against. She had to merely stand and take punch after punch as the magician with too much ego let off steam.

"What do you mean, he's gone?" Alicia asked, racing over to the window.

Plotting Panda glanced around nervously. "He was here, and now he's not."

Alicia shook her head, hurrying back over to the workstation. "Well, then he's gone to fetch his master or something else. I have to focus on getting this ready. I just need another minute."

"I went ahead and fastened the loose wires," Laidback Lion said.

"Thanks," Alicia muttered, trying to figure out where she'd left off.

Something clunked on the roof, and her eyes darted to the side. "That was the wind, right?"

Both robots nodded mechanically.

Another loud clunk.

"The gremlin might be on the roof, then," Alicia said matter-of-factly. "But really, how can he get in?"

"I'm sure he can't," Laidback Lion stated.

"I've calculated at least three possible entrances from the roof," Plotting Panda related.

Alicia glanced up at the ceiling. "Does one involve a skylight?"

The gremlin had his face pressed to the glass, a crazed expression in his large eyes.

Plotting Panda nodded.

"Well, I can't concern myself with him," Alicia said. "I've got seconds to get this working."

"Don't worry, I'm sure he can't get in here," Laidback Lion said.

And then glass rained down from overhead, making Alicia cover her head as the gremlin fell straight into the middle of the room.

"Keep working," Plotting Panda ordered. "We've got this."

He flashed an urgent look at Laidback Lion, who brandished the wrench he was holding and nodded. "It's time for payback for the last several weeks."

Plato knew Liv was in trouble. He could feel it in his bones, the same way he felt his own aches and pains.

They were connected in strange ways.

He knew without knowing how that she was paralyzed. Being assaulted. Out of options.

In cheetah form, he raced through the streets of Venice, sliding around corners. He would have transported to her side, but there was a strange cosmic force at work in Venice that made doing so with any accuracy nearly impossible. This was an odd place for many reasons.

Tourist turned and pointed as they looked out their balcony windows at the large cat splashing through the streets. They'd dismiss him as an overweight alley cat or make up another excuse.

He heard the blunt sounds of skin meeting skin as he veered around the corner. There she was, teetering back and forth after being punched in the face.

A growl full of Plato's vengeance and fury ripped through the night air just before he raced forward.

Alicia had never worked so fast before. She didn't even

know if she was assembling everything the right way. There was no time to second-guess herself or check her measurements.

She tried not to look up when she heard a crash, but too often she did, catching a blur of black and white mixed with gray as Plotting Panda's front rolled into the gremlin. Or orange mixed with gray as Laidback Lion dove off a box, delivering a flying punch to the evil little creature.

Alicia knew Liv was out there racing around Venice, trying to buy her time. She'd hoped to get an update, but the spyware had gone silent, which wasn't good. Either something had happened to Liv, or it was soaked through, which also meant something had happened to Liv.

Taking a steadying breath, Alicia tried to focus as she completed the last part of the electromagnetic device. This was the most crucial step. Fusing the spigot into place was what made this magical tech. It wasn't so much science as it was spell work, and yet it was so much of each that Alicia had to rely on both parts of her: the analytical and the magical.

She rarely thought of herself as a scientific magician, but rather as a magical scientist. It was semantics to some, but to Alicia, it meant something. Like Liv, she existed only to tinker. To fix. To create. And magic was the part of it that enhanced her world. Even without magic, Alicia would still build, invent, and innovate. Without magic, she knew who she was. There weren't many who could say that, because magic was everything to them. They were nothing without it.

That wasn't true for Liv Beaufont, though. Take away

her powers, and she was still a fierce Warrior whom most would regret pissing off.

Alicia flipped up her head as Plotting Panda careened into the front wall. Her mouth popped open, and her heart leapt. She wanted to run to her robot, but in the next second, Laidback Lion nearly hit her in the face as he was tossed through the air.

She heard the overworking of gears as her precious robots tried to get up, but they'd need repairs before they could fight again, and Alicia knew that. This was fine, though, because what she'd do next would take them out completely.

The gremlin stood in the middle of the room, his hands on his hips and his teeth bared. He growled at Alicia, leaning forward like he was about to charge.

She narrowed her eyes at him. Matched his stance. Flipped a switch.

CHAPTER THIRTY

The devices all over Alicia's shop all buzzed once as if coming to life, and then the noise dissipated like a fly slowly dying. One by one, the lights on the various devices flickered and died.

She'd done it!

Liv would have a chance against Shitkphace, especially if she'd worn down his magical reserves.

Alicia didn't have a chance to rejoice or celebrate because the gremlin charged her, his mouth wide open and a high-pitched war-like scream echoing from his mouth.

***

Liv wasn't sure how much she could take. She'd been in some pretty gnarly fights, but in all of them, she'd had the ability to defend herself. Shitkphace wasn't what anyone would call an honorable man. Or person. He fought unfairly, hitting a person when they were incapacitated and repeatedly calling them "little girl" like it was an insult. He was not only responsible for creating holes in the fabric of time, but he had also bruised Liv's face, which would make her look ridiculous at Rudolf's wedding.

She was busy entertaining herself with self-pitying thoughts, which thankfully distracted her from the pain as the magician landed blow after blow on her face. Liv was distracted when she caught something over Shitkphace's shoulder. It was a blur of orangey-brown. The movement of a large cat.

She was relieved that she was about to be rescued, then she stumbled to the side. Her feet worked under her. Her hands moved. She was free.

The figure about to pounce from several yards away froze at Shitkphace's back. The evil magician paused too, tilting his head to the side, probably wondering why his human punching bag was moving on her own.

He reached into his pocket and withdrew the remote. Liv allowed this, working her jaw back and forth, trying to feel normal again although her face and body were throbbing from the beating.

Shitkphace pointed the remote at her. It did nothing.

Liv dragged the back of her sleeve over her face, mopping up the blood streaming from her face. "You would have been better off if the House of Seven had sent Decar Sinclair to take care of you," she said, narrowing her eyes as her hand flew to Bellator at her side. "He would have been nothing for you to deal with. However, Father Time sent me, Liv Beaufont, instead, and although I'm not ruthless like Decar, I don't take a beating lying down."

Momentarily disoriented by the sudden change of events, Shitkphace rapidly slammed his fingers on the buttons of the remote. When nothing happened and Liv withdrew her sword, he shot his palm into the air.

A small gust of wind, not even strong enough to dry her soaked hair, swept through the air.

Liv laughed. "Guess you shouldn't have exhausted your reserves with that fancy flying."

Shitkphace looked ready to piss himself. He stumbled backward, checking over his shoulder. He did a double-take on noticing the cheetah at his back. When he spun to face Liv, there was pure fear and pleading in his eyes.

She brought Bellator up, feeling the hunger of the sword. It wanted justice. It wanted revenge. It wanted to slice through this enemy, sending him to the bottom of the canal.

"You really should have thought before messing with Alicia and me," Liv said as the figure cowered. "Yes, we're only little girls, but we're smart girls—a combination no one should ever underestimate."

Like the coward he was, Shitkphace whipped around and ran.

Liv brought Bellator up in a flash, striking the magician in the back. She didn't like to stab her enemies in the back, but when they ran rather than fight, they left her no options. That was what happened when you dueled with a shitface, she thought, putting Bellator away.

<hr>

Alicia didn't flinch as the gremlin with razor-sharp teeth charged at her. She'd never been taught how to fight, but she knew how to survive, and in many ways, that was the same thing.

Throwing her hand into the air, she directed a blast at the gremlin.

He ricocheted off the walls like a ping pong ball, bouncing around the shop in an attempt to distract her. Alicia kept her eyes on the rapidly moving gremlin, not allowing herself to blink as he soared by her face, screaming in her ears. This had been one of the many tactics the gremlins had used to capture Alicia, subduing her until their master arrived to find her tied up. That was when everything had gone wrong for her. She'd been defeated and her shop taken over. But not this time. No, Alicia wasn't allowing power-hungry villains to mess up her world again, or the place she loved so dearly.

Reaching down, Alicia picked up a loose pipe Laidback Lion had left by the device, thinking it could be helpful for adding extra support. They hadn't needed it, as evidenced by the fact that Alicia's two beloved robots were incapacitated. This time, Laidback Lion leaving tools lying around had been advantageous, even though Plotting Panda always griped about it.

Alicia brought the pipe around the same way she'd seen Liv do in battle and swung it at the blur that passed through the air. The instrument connected like a bat hitting a ball and she followed all the way through, swinging the pipe in a fluid arc. The gremlin flew through the air and crashed through the display window at the front, soaring across the canal, where it smacked into a building. It slid down into the canal and floated away, hopefully realizing it had been defeated by a scientist who was done putting up with the wicked creature's shit.

CHAPTER THIRTY-ONE

Every kill came at a price. Yes, Liv had rid the world of an awful man who cared little for justice, life, or science. However, his blood was on her hands.

Literally.

She cleaned her soiled hands after wiping off Bellator, having kicked Shitkphace's body into the canal, where hopefully he'd do some good, becoming food for the fish.

However, even though she'd done her job, it wasn't easy to kill. It was an act that marked her soul each and every time. Bellator thirsted for the hunt, for the final swing that rid the world of an evil-doer. Liv hadn't gotten to that point yet. She always questioned whether she could have done things differently. Taken Shitkphace into custody. Had his magic locked somehow. There were never any clear answers to these conundrums, though. She'd just have to work them over in her head night after night until she was at peace over the whole thing—not that there was any guarantee a day like that would happen.

"You couldn't have done it any differently," Plato said, having returned to his normal form.

Liv sheathed Bellator and nodded. "Yes, but I could have gotten punched in the face fewer times. I think that jackfruit broke my nose."

She pointed at her face, trying to remember the incantation Hester had taught her for self-mending. Warmth spread over her nose as the spell took effect, suddenly making it easier to breathe again.

"I'm sorry I wasn't there to stop that shitface from pummeling you," Plato said, real remorse in his voice.

Liv shrugged. "You had a job to do. I did, as well. But you showed up."

"And I backed off when I saw you'd been unpaused."

"Thanks for that," Liv stated. "I know you could have saved me, but…"

"You wanted to save yourself," Plato said, finishing her words.

Liv nodded. "This one got a little personal. Not just because of Papa Creola and Alicia, but also for some other reason I'm not entirely sure of."

"Maybe it's because Shitface reminded you of another power-hungry magician, one you feel powerless to stop," Plato offered.

Liv couldn't believe how accurate the observation was. "Yeah, one I feel can deliver blow after blow to me, and I just have to take it."

Plato and Liv stared at the gentle beating of the canal water. It was still rising but would return to normal levels by the time the sun rose.

Feeling her stomach rumble with hunger, Liv finally

shrugged, returning to reality. "I don't know, though. Maybe I've made Adler Sinclair into a villain in my mind. He might just be a grumpy old man who has done nothing wrong other than being a pain in my ass."

"Maybe," Plato replied.

Liv drew a deep breath. "How about we hit a gelato shop after checking on Alicia? Surely one will be open by then."

"If not, I know how to break into one."

Liv gave him a scolding expression. "I really hope Alicia is okay."

"The signal worked," Plato stated. "So I'm sure she's fine."

Glass was everywhere when Liv entered Alicia's shop. She gave Plato a curious glance. "This doesn't look like she's fine."

He gave her a noncommittal expression before disappearing as Alicia rounded the corner from the back of her shop.

Liv almost had the impulse to run to the girl and give her a hug. She stopped herself. "Alicia! Are you okay? The shop."

She glanced around. "It will be fine. And Shitkphace?"

"You never have to worry about him coming after you again and taking your place, or his gremlins," Liv stated.

Alicia held up a metal pipe in her hand and nodded, slapping it into the palm of her hand. "No, I'll never fear gremlins again. They have no power over me."

"Do you want my help cleaning up?" Liv asked, staring around at the wreckage.

"No, but is it safe to turn off the signal?"

"Yeah, I don't see why not," Liv answered.

Alicia ran over to the device in the middle of the room that was broadcasting a low buzzing noise and a great deal of heat. She flipped a switch and it died.

Liv withdrew Bellator when something small and orange stirred at her feet. Alicia slid in front of her, putting an arm across her chest.

"It's okay," Alicia said in a soothing voice. "They are safe."

"They?" Liv asked, and as if cued, something else stirred on the far side of the room. From the rubble, a panda head poked out, one of its eyes looking the wrong way.

Alicia scooped up what Liv realized was a robotic lion, then ran over and grabbed the panda.

"These are yours, I gather?" Liv asked as the scientist put the robots on a workbench. They tried to walk, but bumped into each other and fell down on their sides.

"Yes, and they are in need of repair, but they've survived, which is all that matters," Alicia said a great deal of fondness in her voice.

Liv placed a hand on the girl's shoulder, realizing how much she'd miss her. "We all survived, thanks to your ingenuity."

Alicia offered her a wide smile. "Thanks to your bravery, Warrior Beaufont. I can never thank you enough for what you did to save me."

Liv shook her head. "I don't need your thanks. Just keep doing what you're doing. The magical world needs your technology, but keep it in compliance with House of Seven regulations. Otherwise, some annoying Warrior will show up here and shut you down."

Alicia laughed. "You're the only Warrior I want in my shop. Speaking of which, if you ever need any help with anything that's in my field of expertise, I'm always at your disposal."

Liv smiled. "Actually, my friend John is working on something that has us both stumped. When you're not busy getting your life back together and pecking around this shop, maybe you can help him?"

Alicia shook her head. "Pecking…very funny. And yes, I'd be happy to offer my assistance. Any friend of yours, Liv, is a friend of mine."

CHAPTER THIRTY-TWO

A sword with a ruby-encrusted handle lay next to a suit of armor that would fit a gnome. Other swords from the Dequiem collection hung in display cases around Subner's shop. It was exciting to see how the Fantastical Armory had been transformed now that it had inventory.

Around the shop were actual customers. They browsed the display cases, many of them jingling gold, which kept Subner attentive to them.

When Liv entered, he merely glanced up and pointed to the door at the back. "He's back there in his office."

"Office. Right," Liv stated.

She guessed he was referring to Papa Creola, who, although he was out of hiding, still seemed to be keeping a low profile. He had a lot of enemies, Liv gathered. And she remembered him telling her about how he used to be inundated with requests, which was one reason he had gone into hiding in the first place.

She breezed by the patrons, keeping her head low and covered. Although she'd fixed her nose, her face was still covered in purplish and greenish bruises from the unfair attack by Shitkphace. Once she had a chance, she planned on stopping by to see Hester. The healer had taught her some healing spells but had cautioned against casting too many on herself. Something like fixing a broken nose was okay, but too many spells could go too far. Hester said that it was cosmetic surgery and magicians usually couldn't stop, taking away every imperfection until they overdid it. She'd stated that Liv should just come to her for such things. People were better at healing others, kind of like a stylist was better at doing other people's hair.

Liv was greeted by total darkness when she opened the door to the back. She closed the door behind her and waited a few seconds, hoping her eyes would adjust. They didn't, because it was pitch-black.

Lifting her hand, she created a fireball. A steep staircase descended into a narrow passageway ahead of her.

"Oh, how I love going into dark, unknown places," Liv muttered to herself, testing the first step. It creaked under her weight. It was probably used to holding Papa Creola or Subner's weight, which was easily half of hers. She just hoped they held as she descended.

"My boss couldn't have an office in a commercial building with generic landscaping and a Starbucks across the street," Liv continued to grumble to herself. "Oh no, he's got to work at the bottom of a dark basement in a shop on a street no one knows about."

On her next step, her foot broke through the board. Liv caught herself on the rickety railing but nearly dropped the fireball.

"Let's not burn down the stairs, even if they are shit," Liv said, trying to pull her leg free of where it was stuck.

When she was finally out of the hole, she took each step a little more carefully. Round and round she went, thinking she had to have gone down a dozen or more flights of stairs. The walls were cold stone, and a faint smell of something sweet grew stronger as she descended.

Liv sniffed, thinking the smell was reminiscent of something. Flowers? Gardenias, maybe? No, it was vanilla. The scent hit Liv with a wave of nostalgia. She suddenly got a flash of running through wildflowers as a child. Entering her home with her parents. Cuddling with her mother and reading books. It was unexpected and nearly bowled her over.

When her vision cleared, Liv strangely found herself at the bottom of the staircase, a faint light flickering in the distance. The floor was slippery under her shoes, making her brace herself on the wall. She released the fireball in case she needed both hands and peered ahead.

"Papa Creola?" Her voice echoed several times, ringing in her ears.

Liv continued on, her fingers tight on the wall for support. She felt like the next step could send her to the ground. Strangely, great trepidation rattled around inside Liv, as if she were walking into a dungeon, about to face another villain. The bruises on her face prickled, reminding her of the battle she'd just faced.

The firelight ahead grew brighter, giving a hint of a strange sitting area ahead. The smell of vanilla was almost intoxicating now. Liv took in a deep breath, letting the scent fill her lungs like it was nourishment.

"Papa Creola?" Liv asked again when she made out an armchair in front of a giant fireplace. Above the mantle was a large hourglass.

"Yes, you're almost here," Papa Creola answered. "Come take a seat, Warrior Liv Beaufont."

The light from the fire brightened suddenly and torches on the walls lit, flaring several feet into the air until lowering to small flames. With the help of the light, Liv realized she was in a cave. That explained the slippery floor and chilly air. However, where Papa Creola sat in the large chair, there was also a broad oriental rug, a coffee table, an ottoman, and a leather sofa.

Liv blinked, allowing her eyes to adjust as she took in the details of the room. She noticed that granules of sand in the hourglass were slipping through the bottleneck. However, the amount of sand on the top didn't diminish, and it also didn't build up on the bottom.

"I guess you haven't considered putting an elevator in this joint, have you?" Liv asked, grateful when her feet met the rug. She took a seat on the couch, finding it extraordinarily comfortable.

"Electricity and I don't mix," Papa Creola said, picking up a long pipe from a side table.

"So this is your office," Liv said, staring around. "I expected some bookshelves. Maybe a few pictures of the Big Bang or the birth of civilization, or at least a painting of some deer grazing in a meadow."

Papa Creola lit the end of the pipe with the tip of his finger and blew out a few rings.

Liv waved her hand through the air, fanning away the

smoke. "Hey, *you* may be timeless, but *I'm* not. Can you blow that over there?"

The little gnome offered her a subtle smile. "You won't die from smoke inhalation, Liv. And I don't believe your death will be anytime soon, although multiple factors are in play with your fate that I can't account for. Your path is a tricky one to predict."

"Is this like one of those conversations normal people have with their boss where they discuss their future?" Liv asked. "I haven't made out a five-year plan, but maybe we have to do my performance report first."

"What is it you smell in here?" Papa Creola asked.

Liv drank in the scent. "It's vanilla."

He nodded. "Yes, and what does it bring to mind for you?"

"Memories from my childhood," Liv said, and strangely found herself lying down on the couch, pulling her boots off and resting comfortably.

"Good memories, I suspect?"

Liv nodded, closing her eyes and seeing images flash in her mind. Things she'd forgotten. Her parent's smiling down at her. Rays of sunlight dancing around Sophia as she played in the grass as a baby. Liv sneaking into Clark's room because she couldn't sleep.

"There is a part of you that is timeless," Papa Creola explained. "It doesn't age. It always was, and always will be. That is where your magic comes from. Those memories are tied to that part of you."

"Meaning what?" Liv asked, resting her hands on her chest, feeling it rise and fall as she grew more comfortable.

"Meaning those are your greatest strengths," Papa

Creola answered. "Thinking about those memories will provide you with great power."

Liv's eyes popped open from a sudden thought. "Mortals don't have magic, though."

"That's correct."

"Well, what are their memories tied to? Don't they have a timeless aspect to them?" Liv asked, worry suddenly coating her voice.

"Ah," Papa Creola stated, understanding in his voice. "They used to. Mortals don't have to have magic to be tied to it. It is the fifth element, and the very one they govern."

"I think you just lost me," Liv stated.

"What element do magicians own?"

"Wind," Liv answered at once.

"And gnomes?" he asked.

"Fire, of course," Liv stated. "And fae and elves have water and ice. The giants are in charge of earth."

"Very good," Papa Creola praised. "That's correct. And mortals own the element of magic."

"How is that possible if they can't use magic?" Liv asked, growing more confused.

"Who better to govern magic than the race who isn't affected by it?" Papa Creola asked.

"But mortals can't see magic anymore," Liv stated. "It's been erased for them. The history has been covered up."

"I see you've taken up your parents' crusade," Papa Creola declared proudly.

"Why haven't you been helping with this?" Liv fired back at once, an accusatory quality to her voice.

Papa Creola blew out a plume of smoke. "It isn't my place. The great war was between mortals and magicians.

It is they who must resolve it. And unfortunately, I have my own battles to fight connected to this all."

"Back to my question about mortals," Liv continued. "If they can't see magic, how can they govern it?"

"They can't. Not anymore," Papa Creola stated. "Every year, magic decreases worldwide because of this."

"I don't understand," Liv stated. "I still have my magic."

"Because you have your memories," Papa Creola stated. "You're connected to that timeless aspect of yourself. However, even with that, your magic would fade for you at some point without mortals. If we erase a single race, the element connected to them will eventually fall away. If we kill all the giants, earthquakes will become an hourly occurrence. Wipe out magicians, and the wind will cease to blow. If there were no gnomes, over time, no one would be able to start a fire. You get the idea, right?"

Liv nodded. "I think so. But mortals aren't extinct. They have just been made to forget magic."

"Which is why the element still exists," Papa Creola imparted. "The few mortals who can see it help to keep it alive, but even then, over time, it will fade the longer it is kept hidden from mortals."

This was a lot to process, and yet it made a lot of sense. Liv took a deep breath, enjoying the familiar scent wafting through the air. "Why does it smell like vanilla in here?"

"It doesn't," Papa Creola answered simply. "You simply smell that which triggers your memories. That is the power of the Great Hourglass."

Liv pointed to the large object suspended over the fireplace. "That's it? Is it like a world clock?"

"It is the hourglass of our world," Papa Creola stated.

"When the last granule of sand falls through its bottleneck, time will end for all things."

"It seems like we're doing okay," Liv observed, noticing how neither level changed as the sand sifted through from the top to the bottom.

"I agree," Papa Creola stated. "It does seem like we're okay. Since you stopped Shitkphace, the Great Hourglass has recovered. Not so long ago, it looked quite different than it does now."

"Really?" Liv asked, sitting up and eyeing the instrument more closely. "Like we were running out of time?"

"Yes, and the time-space continuum is a fickle thing," Papa Creola said. "It changes rapidly depending on what happens. When you stopped Shitkphace, things returned to normal."

"I guess you don't need me to run you through what happened in Venice, do you?" Liv questioned.

"I think it's fair to say that I figured it out on my own," Papa Creola said, a hint of laughter in his voice.

"But mortals," Liv stated. "They are separate from this business with time. They relate to magic itself, don't they?"

"Yes, and the longer things continue the way they are, the more risk magic has of disappearing forever," Papa Creola stated. He shrugged. "I guess that wouldn't be the end of the world, but it would be the end of me and Plato and portals, and many other things in your world."

"Then it would be the end of *my* world," Liv said with a sudden realization. Her present world had changed so much from what it used to be. It was all dependent on magic, even if she hadn't realized it then. "What would happen if you ended?"

"There would be chaos," Papa Creola answered. "No repercussions. No laws to time. No ways of fixing problems in the past, present or future."

"So we can't allow anything to happen to magic," Liv said with conviction. "I have to figure out how to fix mortals so they can see magic. I have to find out how to uncover the history."

"I'm afraid, Liv, you have much more to do than that," Papa Creola said, a heavy weight in his voice suddenly. "You have to restore balance to the House. But yes, first you must wake mortals up and recover the lost history."

"Any suggestions on how to do this?" she asked.

"Stay connected to that part of you that is your source of magic," Papa Creola stated.

"Yes, my memories, because that's my power."

"Oh, and it doesn't hurt to have a mortal around you who can see magic," he added.

John, Liv thought. *Of course, he was helping to fuel my magic.*

Was that why her magic was stronger than most? Because she was connected to a mortal who could see magic? Who was possibly one of the mortal Seven?

Liv had so many questions running through her head that she could hardly sit still. She popped up to her feet and began pacing.

"Another question," Liv began.

"Why am I still hiding in a dark basement if I came out of hiding?"

She nodded.

"Because I have an enemy I don't entirely know how to fight," Papa Creola explained.

That admission sent a chill down Liv's spine. She could hardly fathom an entity who gave Papa Creola pause.

"Is this villain more powerful than you?" Liv asked.

"He has powers that are different than mine, and he isn't afraid to take casualties, I believe."

"So you're hiding from him," Liv stated with disappointment. She'd thought Father Time had changed.

"Charging into battle when I don't know what I'm up against isn't very wise," he explained. "I'm more confident than ever that something evil seeks to destroy me so that he can bend the laws of time."

"But wouldn't that ruin time for everyone?" Liv asked.

"It would create chaos, like we spoke about earlier, which for some would allow them to have what they want," Papa Creola stated. "You understand that the world thrives on balance. There is no good without bad. No light without dark. No past without a future. Others don't see this, and think the rules simply hold them back."

"But if we all lived forever or defied time, there would be no justice in the world."

Papa Creola smiled at her, his eyes twinkling. "And that's why you are my first recruit. You intrinsically want what's good for all. Not because it's right. Not because I state it's the law. But rather, because you know it to be what's good and true."

"So, what now?" Liv asked, her anxiety bounding out of her chest. "You've got someone after you. I've got mortals to fix. There's so much to do. But is there another mission that threatens the Great Hourglass?"

Father Time gazed for a long moment at the object over the mantle. He finally shook his head. "Not for now. It's time that you return to the mission that brought you to the House of Seven."

"What brought me to the House was that I had to take on the role as Warrior because Reese and Ian had been murdered or whatever," Liv said, suddenly on edge.

"No, that wasn't what brought you," Papa Creola argued. "Think back. What was it?"

Liv gave it a moment, trying to remember the not-so-long-ago events, although they felt like hundreds of years ago. So much had changed. Liv had changed. "My parents…"

He nodded. "You have done well in your training, making contacts, and fighting as a Warrior. But the time has finally come for you to discover their full story."

"You mean, to find out who murdered them?"

"Knowing the past will be the only way to progress for you in this scenario," Papa Creola explained. "Other things have taken precedence up until this point. The House had missions for you. I had a mission for you. There will be others. However, now it's time you put all of your energy into picking up where they left off."

"The sword…" Liv said, thinking of Inexorabilis.

"Yes, I believe Subner is ready to advise you about your mother's weapon."

CHAPTER THIRTY-THREE

Liv's lungs ached by the time she reached the top of the stairs. She took a few extra moments to catch her breath before she reentered Subner's shop.

"Seriously, that man needs an elevator down to his office," Liv said to the gnome as he hurried over to shut the door to the shop and lock it.

"What did you smell when you were down there?" he asked, pulling the drapes closed.

"Vanilla."

Subner nodded. "That's a good one. I smell homemade chocolate chip cookies."

It was chilling to Liv that everyone was merely a collection of their memories. That those were our powers. And it actually made sense. At the end of the day, all anyone has is time. Possessions and riches and fame matter very little without time. Therefore, it is how we spend it that counts. It is the memories we hold that grant us power.

"So you figured out which guy made my mother's sword?"

"Woman," he corrected.

Once Subner had returned to the counter, he withdrew Inexorabilis, managing the sword with great ease even though it was much bigger than him. "It has taken me more time than I would have thought, but I've been able to determine the maker of the sword. Only she will be able to retrieve the memories your mother locked into the blade."

Based on the intensely serious expression on Subner's face, Liv guessed he didn't have good news for her. "Is the elf dead?"

To her relief, he shook his head. "No, but she does live a great distance from here, in a place that can only be reached through actual travel, not by portal magic."

Liv nodded. "I'd expect no less. I'll have to cross pits of fire and battle cyclops, won't I?"

He lifted a single eyebrow. "Why, yes. How did you know?"

"I'm sort of good about guessing how the gods will design my missions," she stated. "Usually it involves impossible aspects and something humiliating, like carrying around a chicken."

"It makes for good stories if nothing else," Subner said, offering her a rare smile.

"Yes, I'm a riot at dinner parties."

"The maker, an elf by the name of Hawaiki Topasna, is ancient," Subner explained. "She was one of the first to settle the islands in Polynesia. However, she's since gone into hiding."

"Of course she has," Liv said with a sigh.

"Currently, she lives on an island most think is uninhabited, called Lehua," Subner continued.

"But if I cross over a volcano and chant the right phrases she'll appear, right?" Liv asked.

He gave her a questioning look. "No, even then she'll probably avoid you or hex you. It's hard to say."

"My mother couldn't have had a nice, welcoming elf on Roya Lane make her sword, could she?"

"Hawaiki is one of the best sword-makers of her time," Subner offered. "This is evidenced by the craftsmanship. I don't usually admire a sword that isn't gnome-made, but this one is one of the finest I've ever seen. The only sword I would put ahead of it is the giant-forged sword you call Bellator."

Liv's eyes darted to her sword on her belt. There was little reason to argue with Subner about who had made her sword.

"So this Hawaiki," Liv began. "Once I find her—"

"If you can find her," Subner cut in.

"Right," Liv grumbled. "If I can find her, how do I get her to help me?"

"That's a good question," Subner stated. "She's not going to want to get mixed up in what that sword shares."

"Of course, she won't," Liv stated. "That would be too easy."

"I suspect the memories your mother sealed into the sword will have far-reaching effects, or she wouldn't have used what would have been an incredible amount of power to do so."

The words Liv had heard upon picking up the sword on the Matterhorn came back to her—her mother's words: "The future belongs to you, my child. To our family. I have buried memories deep within this sword, and only an expert can uncover them. But be careful. What you discover can't be unlearned, and it will change everything."

"Yes, I believe you're right," Liv said after a long pause.

"I know little about Hawaiki, but I have heard many rumors," Subner stated.

"Like that she prefers dark chocolate over milk and will fold for a box of fresh donuts?" Liv asked.

He shot her a serious expression.

"What?" Liv asked. "I mean, if I lived on a remote island in the middle of nowhere, I'd probably kill for some Krispy Kremes. I'm just saying."

"No, what Hawaiki has long sought after is not something just anyone can provide for her," Subner explained.

"Hey, depending on where you live, it's not easy to get those donuts," Liv stated. "You know there aren't any Krispy Kreme stores in North or South Dakota?"

Subner blinked at her. "That's fascinating information, which I'm certain will be of zero use to me ever."

"Hey, you never know."

"As I was saying, Hawaiki has long desired something," Subner said. "I believe if you can offer it to her, she'll recover the memories and information hidden in the sword."

"Should I guess, or do you just want to tell me?" Liv asked.

"What Hawaiki wants is something rare that most have never seen," Subner went on.

"Yes, yes, I'm sensing the theme here," Liv stated. "Is it expensive too?"

"I do not know the value of these, or even where to look."

"This is on par with the kind of helpful information you offer me. Remember when you wanted me to find your weapons collection but didn't know where I should look or who took them? Oh, that was fun."

Not impressed, Subner pursed his lips. "Hawaiki desires a miniature dragon."

"Oh, cool," Liv said. "So not a regular dragon, which I can't really provide, but specifically a miniature one."

"They are incredibly rare—"

"You've mentioned that," Liv interrupted.

"And they hold powers that normal dragons don't," Subner stated. "Ones that are only unlocked when they bond with their rightful master."

Liv let out a weighty breath, realizing she was going to need to brush up on this subject in *Mysterious Creatures*. She didn't know where she'd find a miniature dragon, only that she would. Somehow…

CHAPTER THIRTY-FOUR

It was strange to find Alicia in John's shop when Liv arrived. Weird in the best way. She was loving the way her life was folding together, the mortals and the Warrior cases. No more were her old life and her new one compartmentalized. They all blended together.

"Yeah, that should be your problem," Alicia said, sliding out from under the pinball machine. Pickles jumped up and licked the scientist's toes, showing his appreciation in a strange way.

"Wow, I never would have found that. Thank you," John said.

Liv winked at him when she arrived beside John. "But you'll know what to look for the next time."

He laughed. "This thing has been a pain in the rear end. There will be no more pinball machines."

"Never say never, Mr. Carraway," Liv said, hugging Alicia, who nearly squealed upon seeing her.

"Thanks for sending me some help, Liv," John said, smiling at the women. "If not for Dr. De Luca, I'm not sure

I could have figured out it was a timing issue with the circuit board."

"You would have figured it out," Alicia said, waving him off. "Although I was happy to help." She glanced around the shop, sighing softly. "And I'm happy to visit this place. There's something so…"

"Perfect about it," Liv supplied.

Alicia nodded. "Yes, that's what I wanted to say, but I didn't want to sound overly presumptuous. I did just enter the place a few minutes ago."

John chuckled nervously. "Well, I like it. Nothing fancy, but it's home to us." He indicated Liv and himself, then his expression shifted suddenly. "I didn't mean to imply, Liv, that it's your… I was simply saying—"

"What this crazy man said," Liv stated. "This is home. And it's utterly perfect."

John beamed.

"Although we *have* done a few magical expansions on the shop, as you might have noticed," Liv stated.

Alicia nodded. "I absolutely did. And I love that John has a non-mechanical helper." She reached down and patted Pickles on the head. The dog was all too excited to accept the attention.

"How are Plotting Panda and Laidback Lion?" Liv asked.

"They are recovering," Alicia stated. "And I should get back to them now."

"Thanks for stopping by," John said, waving like a schoolboy at the magician.

"Actually, I'd love to stop by again if you'll have me," Alicia said, blushing slightly.

"*If* I would?" John asked, clutching his chest. "It would be an honor."

"It's just that I don't encounter many magical-tech shops like this one," Alicia explained.

"Well," John said, combing his hand through his hair, "it's not really supposed to be—"

"What you see is my fault," Liv stated.

"There is no fault," John amended.

"Anyway, it's not like your shop, Alicia," Liv explained. "It wasn't planned to be full of magic-tech. We serve mortals, unlike you."

"I know," Alicia said, rubbing her arms and looking around. "That's one reason I find it so charming. You have a different approach. I love the old appliances. They have been given a second life, and that means—"

"They don't end up in the landfill polluting the Earth," John stated.

"Yes, that's one reason I make my gadgets out of reusable materials," Alicia said. "Actually, if you'd like to discuss some practices, I'd love to tell you about a few of the interesting ones I've found."

"I would love that!" John said cheerfully.

Liv suddenly got the feeling she wasn't really in this conversation. She simply beamed back and forth between the magician and the human, enjoying listening as they exchanged ideas on best practices.

"I should get out of your hair," Alicia said after a minute. "Sorry, I could talk geek all day with you two. I never have anyone who understands this stuff."

"We are your people, then," Liv stated. "You should pop

over any time, especially on the days I have cases. I bet John could use the extra help."

"I wouldn't want to inconvenience Alicia—"

"Consider it an exchange program of sorts," Liv said, cutting John off.

"I'd love that," Alicia said, blushing again. "Liv, I've got to portal out. Can you please follow me to the back, where I think it's best to portal?"

Liv knew it was fine to portal right where she was. She'd done it a hundred times. "Absolutely," she said, leading the scientist to the back.

When they were past the swinging door, Alicia turned around, urgency in her eyes. Liv expected her to say a few different things, but not what she actually said.

"Liv, I swear my magic is stronger now!"

"Now?" Liv questioned.

"Since entering John's shop," she explained.

Liv nodded. That made sense. "Yes. He's a mortal who can see magic."

Alicia gave her a confused expression.

"He is good about enhancing magician's magic," Liv stated, remembering what she'd recently learned.

"Oh, well, I guess that makes sense, although I'm not sure why," she said.

"No worries," Liv replied. "Just come back often to catch up and get the boost to your magic. I think it will be good for everyone."

Alicia threw her arms around Liv's shoulders, squeezing her tight. "I'll definitely be back. I love everything about you, Liv Beaufont. Your giant. Your magician friend named Stefan. Your cat. And your mortal friend."

Liv hugged her back, having no words except, "Me, too."

———

"She used to be a chicken," Liv said, elbowing John in the side when she sidled up next to him after returning from the back.

He laughed. "I'm guessing you're referring to that lovely scientist you had help me with the pinball machine."

"She's a tinkerer," Liv corrected. "Just like us."

He grinned at her. "There is no one like us."

Liv didn't know what to say to that, so she pointed at the pinball machine. "What's wrong with it?"

He indicated the scrap piece of paper. "It's detailed there."

Liv glanced over the analysis and nodded, swirling her finger through the air. A moment later the machine fired to life, the lights blazing and the sounds echoing in the shop. "All fixed. Now pack for Hawaii." Then, thinking of her next mission, she amended, "Actually, you should go to Mexico or Bali or somewhere else."

"Yeah, fine," he acquiesced. "I don't really feel like I earned this vacation. I didn't find the problem, nor fix it."

"John, you've worked tirelessly for decades," Liv argued. "I'd say of anyone, you deserve a vacation."

He hung his head suddenly, heaviness in his movements. "Can I tell you something, though?"

Liv nodded. "What is it?"

"I know you're busy, and I'm not asking you to go with me. I'm just saying, I don't really want to take a trip by myself right now. Maybe in a bit, when it makes sense. I don't know."

Liv understood immediately. John had just taken his life back after Chloe. He had so much more to experience now that he wasn't throwing himself into his work. "You know what? The vacation can wait until you're ready. In the meantime, why don't you just work on what makes you happy, and invite Alicia to the shop to help with things you want?"

"You think she will come?" he asked, a new excitement in his eyes.

"I think if you invited her here for cold tea and stale biscuits, she'd accept," Liv stated.

He laughed. "You sound like a British person."

Liv glanced down at her dirty clothes, realizing she hadn't changed since Venice. "I don't feel like one."

As if cued by her repugnant reaction to her appearance, Clark and Sophia marched through the door, looking as refined as ever in their pressed clothing.

Liv's face spread with joy as Sophia ran over and wrapped her arms around her. Liv didn't have a chance to react before Sophia glanced up, tears welling up in her eyes. "Liv, you have to come back to the House with us. We have something of urgency you have to see!"

CHAPTER THIRTY-FIVE

No one said anything all the way to the House of Seven. Liv kept throwing sideways glances at Clark, but he would only shake his head as if that was the answer to the questioning look in her eyes.

Sophia moved so quickly in her dress covered in red roses that Liv had to speed-walk to keep up with her. This was an emergency, and yet Liv didn't get the impression that either of her siblings was sad. They were anxious, yes. Perplexed, maybe. But not upset. Actually, a couple of times, Liv noticed a slight smirk on Clark's face when he didn't know she was watching him.

Once they were in the House of Seven, Liv didn't know what to expect. Would they go straight to the Chamber of the Tree? Was it the Black Void? Maybe this had all been a trick to try to get Liv to attend a party in one of the ballrooms?

When Sophia led them up the stairs, Liv sped past her, halting at the top of the first landing. "What's going on? Is everything all right?"

Sophia nodded and then shook it. "Yes, but not really."

Clark stepped up even with Sophia. "It isn't worth explaining, and especially not here. The only way to see this is with your own eyes."

"Okay, well, you two have quite the way of unveiling things," Liv stated. "I'm sending you with all news from now on, and you can play this mysterious game with others. It totally catches one off-guard."

Clark took the lead, not stopping until he was at the door for the apartment he shared with Sophia.

Liv was about to follow him in when Sophia grabbed her wrist. Glancing back at her sister, she noticed how serious she seemed.

"Just don't hurt him," Sophia said softly.

"Clark?" Liv asked.

Sophia shook her head. "No. Just keep an open mind until you've heard everything."

Liv didn't know what to say. She swallowed and stepped through the door after Clark.

Once they were in the privacy of the residence, Liv blinked around at the place. It didn't appear any different than usual. On the main wall were the words which always tightened her chest: *Familia Est Sempiternum.*

"What is it?" Liv asked, doing a full turn, trying to figure out if this was a strange trick.

Sophia stepped into the middle of the room and squatted down, the skirt of her dress forming a bell. "It's okay. You can come out now."

Liv wasn't sure what she expected to happen next, but it definitely wasn't this. The door to Sophia's room squealed as it opened all the way. Liv's hand flew to Bellator, and then a small dragon entered the room. At first, Liv thought Sophia's egg had hatched, but then she remembered that it was missing. And this dragon was orange and red, with bright eyes that seemed too mature to belong to a baby. That was when Liv realized that she'd seen this dragon, but only once. It was a miniature that belonged to Adler Sinclair. Liv couldn't believe she'd forgotten about him, and yet, the timing was incredibly uncanny.

"What's he doing here?" Liv asked, watching as Sophia got onto all fours, staring intently at the dragon as it approached. He kept flicking his eyes at Liv and then at Sophia, hesitation in his every move.

When no one answered and the dragon drew closer, Liv pulled Bellator from its sheath. All eyes swiveled to her.

"No," Sophia said in a hush. "He won't harm us. But he wouldn't tell me why he's here until we brought you."

"Wait, you're communicating with that thing?" Liv asked indicating the dragon, who had stopped moving, his head to the side and steam billowing from its nose.

"His name is Indikos," Sophia said. "And yes, I can communicate with him telepathically."

Liv moved so she was between Sophia and the dragon. "Why did he want me here? Actually, how did he get in here in the first place? Is he the one who took your egg?"

Sophia pushed to her feet. "We're not sure. I was in my room when he came out from under my bed. He told me he wanted to help and had important information, but that I had to retrieve you and Clark first."

Liv regarded the dragon with skepticism. "How do we know this isn't a trick and Adler is setting us up? Indikos shouldn't be in here at all."

Clark nodded. "I agree, and have similar concerns. But we can't make any decisions until we at least hear what the dragon has to say."

Liv glanced at Sophia. "Well, she's the one who hears what he says. Can you serve as a translator for us?"

Sophia nodded and knelt on the floor again. She extended a hand to the small dragon. "It's okay. We're all here, and ready to hear what you have to say."

"If you speak to him telepathically, why are you talking out loud?" Liv asked.

Sophia glanced up at her. "It's for your benefit. That way, you at least know what I'm saying. Indikos speaks in my mind, very much the same way that my dragon does."

"So you're a dragon whisperer?" Liv asked.

"According to Bermuda Laurens, all dragon riders have this ability," Sophia explained.

"Cool. Sophia talks to dragons. I talk to chickens and cats, and you, Clark…" Liv paused. "What do you talk to?"

He flashed her a defiant look. "To myself."

"Oh, nice one, brother," Liv commended. "Your comedic timing on that was good."

"I find that if I'm self-deprecating, you appreciate my jokes more," Clark stated. "I'm not sure what that says about you, though."

"That I have a warped sense of humor and you've fallen victim to it," she replied.

Sophia gave them both impatient looks. "If you two are done?"

Liv straightened, flashing Clark a punishing expression. "Yes, I'm ready, if Clark will act serious for once."

"Ha-ha," he said with zero inflection.

Sophia closed her eyes, a serene expression on her face. Liv kept her hand on Bellator, still unsure whether this was a trick or not. Clark shared her paranoia, she realized. He reached back to the entryway, grabbing their father's cane from its resting place.

Sophia's bright blue eyes popped open, and her hand flew to her mouth.

"What is it?" Liv asked, reflexively falling into a fighting stance.

Holding up her hand, Sophia put her at ease. "It was Indikos who helped to steal my dragon's egg."

Liv narrowed her eyes at the miniature dragon. He lowered his chin, suddenly appearing fragile, although that was usually the opposite impression she got when looking at a dragon—not that she'd been around many. Well, none. Just this one. Liv had really only seen dragons in books, which was typical of most people.

"So why is he here saying he's going to help us?" Liv's eyes slid over to Clark. "I think this is a trick."

He nodded, pulling the cane apart to reveal the two small swords inside.

"It's not a trick," Sophia argued. "He has had a change of heart and wants to make things right."

"Well, tell him to get to talking, and fast," Liv stated.

"He understands what you say," Sophia said with a pursed expression. She closed her eyes again. After a long moment, she opened them.

"It was Adler," she said in a whisper.

"Well, I think we all sort of figured that," Liv stated boringly.

Sophia waved her off. "No, Indikos said that Adler came in here to get the egg."

"How, though?" Clark asked. "He can't get into our home. Only a Beaufont can, or someone invited by one of us."

Sophia's eyes closed at once and remained that way. "Adler has a way of bending the rules."

"Again, is anyone really surprised by this information?" Liv asked.

"Can he tell us how he's bending the rules?" Clark asked, starting to pace, a sword in each of his hands. "What rules can he break? What do we need to watch out for?"

Sophia shook her head, her eyes still closed. "Indikos refuses to speak about that."

"Then he better start talking about something else, or I'm giving him back to Adler on the tip of my sword," Liv threatened.

"He says that he didn't want to help Adler locate the egg," Sophia stated.

"How did he even know about it?" Liv asked.

"Remember the prophecy?" Clark asked. "Maybe Adler was aware of it and figured out that it could refer to Sophia."

"That's not it," Sophia said at once. "But again, Indikos doesn't want to talk about some things. He says it's better that way."

"Maybe for him," Liv quipped.

"Where is the egg?" Clark asked.

"Adler has it," Sophia explained. "He took it after Indikos helped him find it. However, he stayed behind because firstly, coming between a dragon and their rider is considered one of their highest crimes. And secondly, he says something dark has been dividing him from Adler for a long time."

"Is this the thing he can't tell us about?" Liv asked, regarding the dragon with a brooding expression.

"He won't say," Sophia answered.

"Shocking," Liv retorted.

"If he's here, then aren't we coming between Adler and his dragon?" Clark asked.

"No," Sophia stated in a definitive tone. "Indikos is no longer bonded to Adler. He says he truly never was. That it was forced."

"I'm still not sure we can trust this old pet of Adler's, even if he states that he isn't loyal to him," Liv said.

Sophia's eyes popped open. "But he says he knows where my egg is and can help me get it back."

"Soph, I'll help you get it back." Liv motioned between her and Clark. "We will do it together. If Adler took it, I'll duel him to the death. I mean, I have been looking for a reason to break his nose anyway."

"You don't understand," Sophia said. "We need Indikos to get into Adler's chamber where the egg is hidden."

Liv rolled her eyes. "That didn't stop Adler from coming in here."

"But we can't bend the rules the same way," Sophia stated. "We need Indikos. He can get in there, and if we go with him, then he'll invite us in."

"Fine," Liv said, sheathing her sword. "Let's go and get this over with."

Sophia shook her head. "Indikos said we can't go yet.

Adler is still in the House of Seven, but he's preparing to leave."

"So, like cowards, we're going to sneak in there and get the egg back?" Liv asked. "Isn't that exactly what Adler did? I vote we march in there and confront the scoundrel."

Clark reached out, placing a calming hand on Liv's shoulder. "Remember that Sophia isn't supposed to have the dragon."

"Says who?" Liv challenged. "Adler? Whoever he has working with him who can bend the rules?"

"It's dangerous to have a dragon, Liv," Clark stated. "You know that. And although it's extraordinary that it magnetized to Sophia, there are many who would challenge it or try to take it from her."

"Okay, so we can't go striding into Adler's chamber and take back the egg," Liv said, a bit defeated.

"Not yet," Sophia amended. "Indikos says he will know when Adler has left, and then he'll help us get in there and take back the egg."

"But Adler is going to know we stole the egg," Liv challenged. "We can't delay the inevitable."

Sophia nodded. "Yes, which is why Indikos has asked a special request for helping us."

"Oh, hold on a second," Liv said, fisting her hands on her hips. "That runt broke into our home and helped Adler steal your egg, but he gets to make special requests?" Liv leveled her gaze on the dragon. "You get that it's a miracle you're still alive right now, right?"

Sophia stood, giving Liv a pleading expression. "He regrets what he did. I don't know how to explain it, but I can feel it with such certainty. He's sincere about that, and about helping us."

"Fine," Liv surrendered. "What does he want?"

"He says that after betraying Adler to get me back my egg, he'll be in great danger," Sophia said.

"Yes, Adler will be on a rampage," Liv said.

Sophia shook her head. "Not from Adler. Apparently, he should be gone for a long time. There's something else in the House that Indikos is frightened of."

"Let me guess, it's the rule-bender," Liv stated.

"I don't know," Sophia answered. "However, Indikos wants our protection in exchange for his help."

"Our protection?" Clark asked. "Won't we all be in danger from whatever this enemy is?"

"I don't know," Sophia stated. "But Indikos has asked that we take him directly out of the House of Seven after he helps. He no longer wants to be here."

Liv's eyes brightened. She couldn't believe the timing. It was uncanny. This was exactly what she needed to persuade the elf to reveal Inexorabilis' secrets. "Yeah, I think I know exactly where we can take him afterward."

"He has to be safe," Sophia argued, facing Liv.

She nodded. "I know I made threats, but I'm serious now. If Indikos helps us, I promise to take him someplace where he won't just be safe, but I suspect he'll be cherished. And as a bonus, he'll help us to unravel a piece of this puzzle so we can finally bring justice to the House of Seven."

dler Sinclair opened the wardrobe in his study, tilting down one way and then the other. When that didn't work, he rummaged through the contents, not finding what he was looking for. Overwhelmed by frustration and grief, he picked up the clothes inside and slung them across the room. The wardrobe was mostly empty now.

"Indikos!" he yelled, his face flushing red. "Where are you?"

Breathless, he turned around to survey the destruction he'd done to his quarters. It was time that he leave. The God Magician wouldn't allow him to delay one more day. But Indikos had gone missing. Adler kept expecting him to turn up, thinking that maybe he'd gone far off to hunt. But something told him at his core that the small dragon was in the House.

His eyes fell on the box sitting on the top of his desk. The one that contained Sophia Beaufont's dragon's egg. He considered taking that with him to the Matterhorn, but he knew it was a bad idea. The climb was steep and dangerous, and once he got up there, there'd be much work to be done.

Adler shook his head. No, he'd just have to leave the egg behind. Indikos, too.

He hadn't wanted to leave the House of Seven at all. He couldn't remember the last time he had for such a long stretch. This was his home. But he knew the God Magician was right. They needed to protect the signal. Decar had to protect the history they'd erased. He was closer than ever to doing that. No giant would be successful against him. And then, once everything was safe and the One had reached full strength, they could take over as the rightful heirs of the House of Seven, reigning with supreme authority.

Of course, the God Magician would have to take out Father Time first. He was the one who stood in the way of Talon fully rising. But he only needed a little longer to increase his strength before he could battle the gnome.

Talon had been disappointed in Adler when he couldn't locate Father Time. He had tried, following Olivia Beaufont, but never able to find out where she went. In the end, the God Magician believed that Adler was stalling about going to the Matterhorn, and ordered him to abandon the job of finding Father Time and continue with the mission as planned.

Adler let out a weighty sigh. He didn't want to leave the House of Seven. He didn't want to leave Indikos behind. And he was fearful what would happen to Talon without Adler to control him and keep him from acting out.

He picked up his bag and slung it over his shoulder,

glancing one last time behind him at his quarters, a small hope fluttering in his chest that Indikos would be there, waiting to take the journey with him.

He wasn't.

Adler swallowed his disappointment and opened the door, charging out into the corridor. He couldn't help feeling that he might never see the House of Seven again.

However, Adler knew that was absurd. It was only that everything was riding on what happened next.

Someone had gotten close to the signal broadcasting from the Matterhorn. If something happened to that, everything would be lost. Everything they had worked for. Mortals would wake up and see magic, and then the old war would inevitably start again. They'd try to rule over magic, governing it, when that was never their place. They'd ruin everything, as they'd tried to do before. That was how the Great War had started.

That was why Adler didn't just plan on guarding the signal broadcasting from the Matterhorn that kept mortals from seeing magic. He planned on increasing its intensity. He hadn't told Decar or Talon about that, but he believed he now possessed the right formula to change the signal so that it prevented mortals from ever coming into power in the House of Seven again.

If what Adler planned worked, the signals would wipe out all mortals forever.

CHAPTER THIRTY-SEVEN

It hadn't been Liv's idea for Sophia to tag along as she and Indikos broke into Adler's quarters. However, the young magician had been persistent. She'd brought up excellent points about how it was her dragon's egg they were going to retrieve. And she should also be there to speak with Indikos, since she was the only one who could.

In the end, Liv couldn't argue with her little sister. It was just that whatever power Adler was pulling on to bend rules in the House of Seven worried Liv even more than usual. The House had been constructed using specific laws. That was how they maintained the balance and order. If there was something present that allowed Adler to bypass the rules, well, it meant they had other things to worry about.

Liv consoled herself with the idea that Adler was gone. Maybe whatever power he was using had left with him. She tried to convince herself that things were looking up. Adler was out of her hair. His dragon had turned on him.

She'd use Indikos to get Hawaiki Topasna to help her with the sword, and then she'd stop the signal on the Matterhorn, find the Mortal Seven, and throw a big party. The end.

She almost wanted to slap her hands together to celebrate the finality of it all. However, deep in her core, Liv knew things weren't going to be that simple. They never were.

"He says it's this door," Sophia said in a hushed voice, pointing to a door in the long corridor.

"Cool," Liv said matter-of-factly, as if her sister telepathically communicating with a dragon wasn't a big deal at all. "Does he have to open the door, or what?"

Sophia lowered her chin, giving Liv an expression that said, "Come on, get real."

"Oh, so we open the door, which allows us entrance because we're with the dragon, right? Kind of like knowing the right guy at a club, huh?" Liv asked.

The miniature dragon was riding on Sophia's arm, his wings half-cocked like he might take flight at any moment. She set her fingers on the door handle and looked at Indikos carefully.

Liv wasn't sure what exchanged between the two of them, but a moment later Sophia returned her gaze to the door and pushed it open. It hesitated for only a moment before opening all the way.

Liv stepped around her sister and Indikos, her hand protectively on Bellator as she scanned the area. As the dragon had told her by way of Sophia, Adler wasn't there. However, it appeared that someone had ransacked the place in his absence.

"Are we late?" Liv asked as Sophia shut the door behind them. "Has someone already searched his quarters for the egg or whatever else?"

The young magician closed her eyes and then shook her head. "Indikos believes Adler did this, searching for him before he left."

"Oh," Liv said, scanning the area. "I do the same thing to my place when I'm about to go on a trip. That's the only way I can find all my undies and matching socks."

Sophia snickered and then glared at the small dragon. "It wasn't a bad joke. I think she's funny."

"Tell the dragon that if he doesn't like that joke, I've got a dozen more he'll loathe," Liv stated, toeing some books on the floor.

"You just did," Sophia said as Indikos flew to a large desk at the back of the room.

As if magnetized, Sophia strode in its direction, her eyes unblinking.

"Soph?" Liv asked, watching her sister robotically move forward.

On the surface of the desk was a large box with intricate detailing. Indikos stood beside it, his eyes intense as he regarded the box.

Liv hurried over, pulling Bellator from its sheath. She wasn't sure what they'd find, but she wasn't taking any chances. Although she didn't know how this could be a trick, she wasn't ready to let down her guard.

"Is that..." Liv's voice trailed away as she peered over Sophia's shoulder.

Her sister nodded. "Yes. I can feel him."

Carefully, Sophia opened the box and there, as bright

and sparkling as Liv remembered, was the large blue drag-on's egg.

As if meeting an old friend, Sophia scooped it up into her arms, cradling it against her chest. She closed her eyes and pressed her cheek to the egg.

Liv waited for a long moment until her sister straight-ened, opening her eyes. "He missed me."

Liv smiled. "Of course, he did. He'd be crazy not to."

Sophia's eyes welled with tears. Liv reached out and grabbed her arm, worried that something was wrong. "What is it?"

Regarding the egg in her arms intensely, Sophia said, "He's close to hatching. He says he was only waiting for me to find him."

Liv kept her eyes glued to the egg as if expecting the small dragon to break free at any moment. When nothing happened, Liv said, "How much longer?"

Sophia shook her head. "Not long, but it's hard to tell. Time works differently for dragons."

Liv nodded like this made sense. "Well, you have him now, and can take him home."

Sophia shook her head. "No, he says it isn't safe there. Adler knows I have him. He might come back for him."

Liv realized she should have expected this. "Then where can we keep him?"

Sophia glanced up, her eyes begging. "Can he stay at your place?"

Liv was already shaking her head before Sophia finished her question. "It's not safe. There aren't the right wards on the place, and you need to be with him. You know Clark would never go for it."

"Clark knows I'm unsafe in the House, especially after this incident," Sophia stated. "He's actually at your place right now setting up proper security."

Liv lowered her chin, realizing she'd been had. "So you two have been planning this?"

Sophia shrugged guiltily. "I'm sorry, but it's for the best. There's no other better place than John's shop. He's a Mortal Seven, like you told me, and you're a Warrior everyone fears."

"Who also has a ton of enemies," Liv added.

"Please, Liv," Sophia pleaded. "Just until he hatches and we figure out something else. You won't even be there."

Liv was about to ask where she'd be, but then there was flapping and Indikos landed on her shoulder. She regarded the small dragon with an annoyed expression. "Oh, that's right, I'm taking this guy to his new home."

To her surprise, the dragon affectionately pressed his head into the space between her neck and shoulder, folding his wings in tight to his body.

This was all unexpected. Indikos changing his loyalty, the solution to getting Hawaiki's compliance, Sophia and her egg, and also the strange fullness in Liv's heart.

It might not have been an ideal situation, but deep down, Liv felt like they were on the right path. There was still much danger ahead of them, but she'd willingly face it for more moments like this.

It was magic that made these things possible. Without it, there would be no dragons hatched. No small magicians changing the world. And no unexpected unfolding of events.

And that meant Liv had to wake the mortals up and

make them see what they'd lost to preserve magic for all. She had to finish what her parents had started.

Sighing deeply, she nodded. "Yes, you and the egg can stay with me."

Sophia almost yelped with joy but stopped herself.

Liv smiled. "But if that dragon is about to hatch, you better start thinking of a name for it."

Sophia nodded appreciatively. "I have a few in mind, but I want to wait until we formally meet. And I promise I won't be a burden. You won't even know I'm at your place."

Liv shook her head at her little sister. "You've never once been a burden. Just the opposite. And remember, I won't be there. Indikos and I have a mission. As promised, I'll be taking him to a place where he'll be safe, and maybe even happy."

The dragon's appreciation poured through him into Liv. It was strange how she could almost feel his thoughts through his actions. She began to understand how Sophia could communicate with him, although she communicated with the dragons on a different level.

Sophia giggled at the exchange. "He's no chicken, but I think he'll make an excellent traveling companion for you. Just promise to return safely from the journey and come back to me."

Liv laughed too. "Don't worry, Soph. Nothing in this world will keep me from returning home to you."

Even though she was standing in Adler Sinclair's chamber and facing another dangerous journey, Liv's heart was bursting with gratitude. She couldn't believe how much her life had changed, and she wasn't going to trade it for anything in the world.

Magic had made her life so much fuller than she had ever imagined it would, and she was going to do everything she could to preserve it forever.

SARAH'S AUTHOR NOTES

JUNE 8, 2019

In the notes for the last book, I discussed how I got the idea for the chicken. Inspiration is a funny thing. I'd channeled my frustrations about having to watch my ex-husband's chicken into a book. Little did I know that I'd actually grow to enjoy the character of the chicken. Don't think I've softened up and I'm going to volunteer to watch my exe's flea bags. Oh no. It's just that I like the idea of turning the negative into a positive. More of that happened with this book.

I had the privilege of getting to spend a week in Italy this spring. To make it even better, Jurgen Moders, beta reader, first proofer and idea swapper, offered to meet me in Rome. To say I was honored was an understatement. Jurgen traveled for twenty-four hours, one way, so that we could meet in person and explore the Coliseum and Forum together. I think there are less chaotic places we could have met, but where would the fun in that be!

We had a lovely time gaining all sorts of inspiration as we strolled through the ancient ruins. But little did we know that the inspiration would come from such unexpected things. We were going through security and the guard kept giving Jurgen crap for the bag attached to his belt. The other guards had said it was sufficient to just look inside but this one wanted it to go through the scanner, which meant Jurgen had to take it off, which meant he had to take off his belt and nearly lose his pants. It was quite the ordeal. I did not laugh. I also was of no help. But afterwards, I did include the scene in the book, sort of, although Liv didn't lose her pants. That's how we turn the frustrating moments into entertainment though.

Thanks to Jurgen for venturing so long to meet up with me. It was such a fun adventure. I then went onto Venice where I kept thinking of all the awesome fight scenes I could construct in the canals. And that's why we have a book set in Italy. The next book is set in Hawaii and therefore you might wonder if I have a trip planned there. The answer is no, but I'm doing a reverse osmosis sort of thing. If I write about it, maybe I'll magically land a trip there. Go there in the mind and you can go there in the body. Hey, magic is real!

Lydia and I often construct story ideas in the morning over breakfast. One morning she or I or the cat said something about a guy named Kyle Foggerbottom. I think we were talking about how Finely, the cat, had to get ready for his accounting job. We go through this every morning talking about how he better get his suit on and get down to the bus stop or he'll be late.

Lydia packs him a candy bar for his lunch because she's one of "those" moms. Shame, shame. Then we talk about how he (the cat) doesn't like Molly in marketing because she teases him but he likes Kyle because he shares his fries at lunch. My cat makes bad food choices.

Anyway, after we'd dialogued about the cat's fake life, one of us gave Kyle a last name. Kyle Foggerbottom. And then I was like, I'm putting a Foggerbottom in my next book. And then I went to the Facebooks and told the fans and they supplied me with lots of first names for Foggerbottom.

And now I'm to my point! Thanks to Jael Sheppard for helping name Phil Foggerbottom. I randomly chose and she was the winner. There were so many great suggestions! Thanks to the rest of the LMBPN "Ladies" for great ideas. Oh and thanks to Deb Mader's for the idea on the Brownie Union.

I swear you all could write the books for me!

Okay, I'm going to go and harass the cat about doing my taxes. Is it any a wonder that I put a talking cat in this book? I've got issues…

JUNE 13, 2019

THANK YOU for not only reading this story but these *Author Notes* **as well.**

(I think I've been good with always opening with "thank you." If not, I need to edit the other *Author Notes*!)

RANDOM (*sometimes*) THOUGHTS?

Amadeus Bucker, Vampire Trucker.

So, walking through a large truck stop-type location in New Mexico, I'm not thinking hard (obviously) when the concept for a new vampire character comes into mind.

A Vampire Trucker.

He would have to have a partner who can handle the sun, and he would have a special area in the back sleeping cab.

Or would it be her?

Would I have the vampire be a vampire with a guy for the daytime? Or, what if it was a pair of twin ladies?

One lady recently "killed," and her sister is a trucker.

So, they look alike. Now, the new vampire trucker

sister has to learn how to handle the road when her sister (who has been running and gunning the blacktop for years) has to deal with her sister intruding in her life?

This is how stuff happens with the creation of new characters.

Why?

Because I don't have a cat. I can't ask it for suggestions.

I'm over fifty years old and I've NEVER owned a cat. There is no room in my life for a four-legged "master-slave" relationship.

Especially one that might bring me rat sacrifices in the morning. (You can keep the sacrifices meant for you to prepare them, Sarah!)

AROUND THE WORLD IN 80 DAYS

One of the interesting (at least to me) aspects of my life is the ability to work from anywhere and at any time. In the future, I hope to re-read my own *Author Notes* and remember my life as a diary entry.

Hwy 40 between Albuquerque New Mexico and Arizona

Just stopped at a rather sketchy gas station / convenience store for an important break.

Picked up a blue Slush Puppy (went to ice too fast), and the mountains in the distance are beautiful as we drive down the road heading back to Vegas.

The cops are pretty heavy here in New Mexico (didn't see any in Texas traveling through the Panhandle), and it's getting on into the evening. Probably have to figure out a place to sleep in a little while.

Well, make that right after I finish these *Author Notes*.

We are sliding through Gallup, New Mexico.

By the time you read this, I'll be back in Las Vegas. We've decided to drive on through since I wrote that sentence two paragraphs back.

I hope you have a fantastic weekend (or week), and may you see a pixie next time you go walking near some trees!

FAN PRICING

$0.99 Saturdays (new LMBPN stuff) and $0.99 Wednesday (both LMBPN books and friends of LMBPN books.) Get great stuff from us and others at tantalizing prices.

Go ahead. I bet you can't read just one.

Sign up here: http://lmbpn.com/email/.

HOW TO MARKET FOR BOOKS YOU LOVE

Review them so others have your thoughts, and tell friends and the dogs of your enemies (because who wants to talk to enemies?)... *Enough said ;-)*

Ad Aeternitatem,

Michael Anderle

ACKNOWLEDGMENTS

SARAH NOFFKE

My favorite part of writing any book is creating the acknowledgements page. It reminds me that writing a book is not a solo task. I might sit alone and write, but the finished product is a result of the support and encouragement of a tribe of people.

Thank you to the readers who buy the books, read them, review and recommend. YOU are the one who keeps us writing. I'm always inspired by the messages I receive from readers. Thank you supporting the books and offering so much richness to my life.

Thank you to my LBMPN family for all the support. Steve, Michael, Lynne, Moonchild, Jennifer and so many others who help champion the book to publication and beyond.

Thank you to the beta readers who offered so many valuable insights early on. Thank you to John, Chrisa, Kelly, Martin and Larry.

Thank you to the JIT team for all the awesome feedback. A new series is always exciting and nerve-wracking.

Michael and I thought we had a great idea for a new world, but we don't really know until we get objective feedback. What would I do without all you awesome readers?

Thank you to my friends and family. Writing is a strange profession. I work weird hours, talk to myself, have a strange diet, get antsy about deadlines. But the wonderful people in my life continue to show their encouragement and thoughtfulness no matter what. It is never lost on me because I know that I wouldn't be doing what I love without all you amazing people, cheering me on.

And as with all my books, the final thank you goes to my muse, Lydia. I wrote my first book so that I could make my daughter proud, and it's never stopped. I write every book for you, my love.

Sarah Noffke writes YA and NA science fiction, fantasy, paranormal and urban fantasy. In addition to being an author, she is a mother, podcaster and professor. Noffke holds a Masters of Management and teaches college business/writing courses. Most of her students have no idea that she toils away her hours crafting fictional characters. www.sarahnoffke.com

Check out other work by Sarah author here.

Ghost Squadron:

Formation #1:

Kill the bad guys. Save the Galaxy. All in a hard day's work.

After ten years of wandering the outer rim of the galaxy, Eddie Teach is a man without a purpose. He was one of the toughest pilots in the Federation, but now he's just a regular guy, getting into bar fights and making a difference wherever he can. It's not the same as flying a ship and saving colonies, but it'll have to do.

That is, until General Lance Reynolds tracks Eddie down and offers him a job. There are bad people out there, plotting terrible things, killing innocent people, and destroying entire colonies. **Someone has to stop them.**

Eddie, along with the genetically-enhanced combat pilot Julianna Fregin and her trusty E.I. named Pip, must recruit a diverse team of specialists, both human and alien. They'll need to master their new Q-Ship, one of the most powerful strike ships ever constructed. And finally, they'll have to stop a faceless enemy so powerful, it threatens to destroy the entire Federation.

All in a day's work, right?

Experience this exciting military sci-fi saga and the latest addition to the expanded Kurtherian Gambit Universe. If you're a fan of Mass Effect, Firefly, or Star Wars, you'll love this riveting new space opera.

NOTE: If cursing is a problem, then this might not be for you.

Check out the entire series here.

The Precious Galaxy Series:

Corruption #1

A new evil lurks in the darkness.

After an explosion, the crew of a battlecruiser mysteriously disappears.

Bailey and Lewis, complete strangers, find themselves

suddenly onboard the damaged ship. Lewis hasn't worked a case in years, not since the final one broke his spirit and his bank account. The last thing Bailey remembers is preparing to take down a fugitive on Onyx Station.

Mysteries are harder to solve when there's no evidence left behind.

Bailey and Lewis don't know how they got onboard *Ricky Bobby* or why. However, they quickly learn that whatever was responsible for the explosion and disappearance of the crew is still on the ship.

Monsters are real and what this one can do changes everything.

The new team bands together to discover what happened and how to fight the monster lurking in the bottom of the battlecruiser.

Will they find the missing crew? Or will the monster end them all?

The Soul Stone Mage Series:

House of Enchanted #1:

The Kingdom of Virgo has lived in peace for thousands of years...until now.

The humans from Terran have always been real assholes to the witches of Virgo. Now a silent war is brewing, and the timing couldn't be worse. Princess Azure will soon be crowned queen of the Kingdom of Virgo.

In the Dark Forest a powerful potion-maker has been murdered.

Charmsgood was the only wizard who could stop a

deadly virus plaguing Virgo. He also knew about the devastation the people from Terran had done to the forest.

Azure must protect her people. Mend the Dark Forest. Create alliances with savage beasts. No biggie, right?

But on coronation day everything changes. Princess Azure isn't who she thought she was and that's a big freaking problem.

Welcome to The Revelations of Oriceran. Check out the entire series here.

The Lucidites Series:

Awoken, #1:
Around the world humans are hallucinating after sleepless nights.

In a sterile, underground institute the forecasters keep reporting the same events.

And in the backwoods of Texas, a sixteen-year-old girl is about to be caught up in a fierce, ethereal battle.

Meet Roya Stark. She drowns every night in her dreams, spends her hours reading classic literature to avoid her family's ridicule, and is prone to premonitions—which are becoming more frequent. And now her dreams are filled with strangers offering to reveal what she has always wanted to know: Who is she? That's the question that haunts her, and she's about to find out. But will Roya live to regret learning the truth?

Stunned, #2
Revived, #3

The Reverians Series:

Defects, #1:
In the happy, clean community of Austin Valley, everything appears to be perfect. Seventeen-year-old Em Fuller, however, fears something is askew. Em is one of the new generation of Dream Travelers. For some reason, the gods have not seen fit to gift all of them with their expected special abilities. Em is a Defect—one of the unfortunate Dream Travelers not gifted with a psychic power. Desperate to do whatever it takes to earn her gift, she endures painful daily injections along with commands from her overbearing, loveless father. One of the few bright spots in her life is the return of a friend she had thought dead—but with his return comes the knowledge of a shocking, unforgivable truth. The society Em thought was protecting her has actually been betraying her, but she has no idea how to break away from its authority without hurting everyone she loves.

Rebels, #2
Warriors, #3

Vagabond Circus Series:

Suspended, #1:
When a stranger joins the cast of Vagabond Circus—a circus that is run by Dream Travelers and features real magic—mysterious events start happening. The once orderly grounds of the circus become riddled with hidden threats. And the ringmaster realizes not only are his circus and its magic at risk, but also his very life.

Vagabond Circus caters to the skeptics. Without skeptics, it would close its doors. This is because Vagabond

Circus runs for two reasons and only two reasons: first and foremost to provide the lost and lonely Dream Travelers a place to be illustrious. And secondly, to show the nonbelievers that there's still magic in the world. If they believe, then they care, and if they care, then they don't destroy. They stop the small abuse that day-by-day breaks down humanity's spirit. If Vagabond Circus makes one skeptic believe in magic, then they halt the cycle, just a little bit. They allow a little more love into this world. That's Dr. Dave Raydon's mission. And that's why this ringmaster recruits. That's why he directs. That's why he puts on a show that makes people question their beliefs. He wants the world to believe in magic once again.

Paralyzed, #2

Released, #3

Ren Series:

Ren: The Man Behind the Monster, #1:

Born with the power to control minds, hypnotize others, and read thoughts, Ren Lewis, is certain of one thing: God made a mistake. No one should be born with so much power. A monster awoke in him the same year he received his gifts. At ten years old. A prepubescent boy with the ability to control others might merely abuse his powers, but Ren allowed it to corrupt him. And since he can have and do anything he wants, Ren should be happy. However, his journey teaches him that harboring so much power doesn't bring happiness, it steals it. Once this realization sets in, Ren makes up his mind to do the one thing that can bring his tortured soul some peace. He must kill the monster.

Note This book is NA and has strong language, violence and sexual references.

Ren: God's Little Monster, #2
Ren: The Monster Inside the Monster, #3
Ren: The Monster's Adventure, #3.5
Ren: The Monster's Death

Olento Research Series:

Alpha Wolf, #1:
Twelve men went missing.

Six months later they awake from drug-induced stupors to find themselves locked in a lab.

And on the night of a new moon, eleven of those men, possessed by new—and inhuman—powers, break out of their prison and race through the streets of Los Angeles until they disappear one by one into the night.

Olento Research wants its experiments back. Its CEO, Mika Lenna, will tear every city apart until he has his werewolves imprisoned once again. He didn't undertake a huge risk just to lose his would-be assassins.

However, the Lucidite Institute's main mission is to save the world from injustices. Now, it's Adelaide's job to find these mutated men and protect them and society, and fast. Already around the nation, wolflike men are being spotted. Attacks on innocent women are happening. And then, Adelaide realizes what her next step must be: She has to find the alpha wolf first. Only once she's located him can she stop whoever is behind this experiment to create wild beasts out of human beings.

Lone Wolf, #2
Rabid Wolf, #3
Bad Wolf, #4

BOOKS BY MICHAEL ANDERLE

For a complete list of books by Michael Anderle, please visit:

www.lmbpn.com/ma-books/

All LMBPN Audiobooks are Available at Audible.com and iTunes

To see all LMBPN audiobooks, including those written by
Michael Anderle please visit:

www.lmbpn.com/audible

CONNECT WITH THE AUTHORS

Connect with Sarah and sign up for her email list here:

http://www.sarahnoffke.com/connect/

You can catch her podcast, LA Chicks, here:

http://lachicks.libsyn.com/

Connect with Michael Anderle and sign up for his email list here:

Website: http://lmbpn.com

Email List: http://lmbpn.com/email/

Facebook:
www.facebook.com/TheKurtherianGambitBooks

www.ingramcontent.com/pod-product-compliance
Lightning Source LLC
Chambersburg PA
CBHW050236110726

47898CB00007B/2175